SHE'S A HOT CHRISTMAS MESS

A BETTING ON CHRISTMAS ROMANTIC COMEDY

SOFIA AVES

CONTENTS

Foreword   5

Chapter 1   7
Chapter 2   18
Chapter 3   29
Chapter 4   31
Chapter 5   40
Chapter 6   49
Chapter 7   56
Chapter 8   65
Chapter 9   73
Chapter 10   85
Chapter 11   95
Chapter 12   111
A Note About Alpacas   117
Betting on Christmas Collection   119
Betting On Christmas   121
READ KING, Z BOYS   123

About the Author   133

First Edition

Published by Little Quail Press

Editing by Partners in Crime

ISBN 978-1-922448-67-5

for all the alpacas without Santa hats who want one
Get one. You deserve it.

CHAPTER 1

FORD

I STOOD in the middle of 57th and West 58th Street next to an alpaca wearing a Santa hat. Fortunately, it wasn't a spitty day, otherwise the local NYC population would be covered in the regurgitated green stuff that hung around Pickles' neck. That alpaca was accurate at a good twenty paces like a showdown gunslinger at high noon.

So far, only two yellow taxis wore his wrath at the limit of his range.

I pulled up the map app on my phone–try saying that ten times fast–scrolling through the streets that showed up, but there was no sign of any Plaza Hotel I could see, despite knowing it existed. The building was a pre-prohibition landmark, and I still couldn't locate it no matter how many blocks I walked in any direction.

Currently, my luck was divided into an eight block radius, and growing alongside my impatience with myself to navigate a city. *The desert is easier to locate than this.* I swore I was getting farther and farther away from my destination, and my own alpaca hooves ached. Pickles nuzzled at his lucerne bucket, but it slid so far down his camelid neck that he couldn't reach the thing. His plaintive honk alerted me to his plight.

"You're not going to starve, big fella." I reached around him, fixing the slim aluminium handle to his Christmas harness, the metal glinting dully against the red and green twists. Pickles dived into the bucket with the renewed fervor of a desperate camel. His Santa hat slipped sideways, and I caught the fluffy thing before it hit the grimy nondescript slush at my feet.

"It had to be snowing for this damn wedding," I muttered, dangling the Santa hat between my fingers.

Not that the wedding was mine; I was in town for an old friend's celebration who I roomed with at Columbia in my early twenties on an exchange program. That had been an alpacalypse of its own, and this trip had the same makings to it already, before I headed back to Western Australia to the largest herd of alpacas and vicuna in my home country.

Somewhere along the line, I thought that bringing my prime breeding stock to the States and double dipping for this trip was a good idea, but a month after arriving, I realised just how impossible it was to house an alpaca in a cityscape at Christmas.

I grumbled away under my breath, flicking the Santa hat against my fingers. Men stuffed with pillows and dressed in similar costumes to Pickles decorated every corner I passed, all with no Plaza Hotel appearing miraculously in front of me.

Pausing near a green grocer shop, I leaned back against the painted glass with its cheery Christmas messages scrawled in three languages. Pickles stopped next to me and grunted softly.

The Santa hat dipped in my hands as a fistful of change and some notes tugged at the material.

"Cute." A rugged-up couple wearing matching ugly sweaters with a small child stuffed into a puffer jacket star suit and mittens paused in front of us. "Can we get a picture?"

I stared at the couple, and then at the proffered child lifted at chest height. "Oh. No. I'm not busking," I assured them.

"It's just one photo, *mate.*" The father put on an atrocious Australian over his New Yorker twang. "One selfie with the llama."

"Alpaca," I corrected softly.

"Whatever." He cackled a little, his eyes wide in that slightly crazed look parents get around this time of year in a bid to do anything to prevent their offspring melting down in a seasonal tantrum.

From the way the lowered child stomped around and rested his forehead wearily against Pickles' foreleg, I suspected he would shortly join those squalling ranks.

I gritted my teeth, and forced a smile. "He can stand next to Pickles."

"Pickles!" the kid screeched, gender unknown, in the suit that consumed the tiny body except for his nose, half frozen mouth, and a pair of eyes peering up. Mood forgotten, the child bounced off the icy slush and grabbed at Pickles' chest fuzz.

Pickles lowered his head and touched his nose to the boy, whuffling curiously. The kid tugged harder.

"Super cute."

The parents backed up a step as a low growl that shouldn't be possible emanated from Pickles' throat. I watch the small bead actively travel the three feet up his long straight neck from one of his four stomachs, and put out my hand a moment too late.

"No, you damn beast. Best back off– gah." I cursed into the palm I slapped over my face as Pickles sprayed the parents with the stinking green contents of his stomach and sent me a victorious side-eye.

"Shit." The father wasn't quite so discreet.

"Trouble. Big trouble, fella." I wrapped my arm around Pickles' neck, pulling him forcefully up before he could divulge the contents of the other three onto the child who managed to miss the spray pattern, still dangling from Pickles' manly chest fuzz.

The pungent scent of marinated lucerne mixed with hotdogs from the stand half a block away in a heady scent that wouldn't be leaving my nostrils any time soon.

The father bellowed with laughter like Pickles' spit was the best thing he had ever seen, while the wife attempted to pick pieces of gooey grass from her hair. Oblivious, the child chuckled, attacking Pickles in his star suit and bouncing off his fleece, his attention already drawn to the next shiny thing along the block.

"Thanks." An extra note was added to my Santa hat.

I shook my head, refusing to deny I wasn't collecting any longer. "That's not gonna come off easily," I assured the mother, who picked furtively at her fleecy jumper.

She sent me a slightly horrified look and skittered off after her family.

Tightening my bearhug around Pickles, I drew him a little closer until we were side-eye to side-eye—there was no chance I'd get within his spitting range—and spoke softly into his ear. "Cute display. Don't do it again, or I'll add lights to your halter, and a candy cane basket for the kiddies. Are we clear?"

Pickles whuffled at me and stuck his nose in his feed bucket.

I rolled my eyes. Of course he was hungry after emptying his last meal onto the local populace.

I checked the directions again, trying to work out my bearings when the one-way alleys didn't seem to line up with anything on my map app. *Damn thing is at least a decade out of date.* Finally, I shoved my phone into my pocket and headed to the nearest intersection.

A man wearing several coats and smelling like last year's roast sat on the ground near the corner looked at me through squinted eyes, but as I approached I realised how glassy they were.

"Want a treat for your animal?" He lifted a candy bucket and a flask full of what smelled like whiskey.

"Thanks," I looked around. "I'm looking for the Plaza Hotel."

"The what?" He rose unsteadily and coughed in my face, his words blurring into the next. One hand cupped around his ear, though he didn't look old enough to be wearing a hearing aid.

"Plaza Hotel," I spoke to him like he was a Martian, and for all the recognition across his face, he may as well have been one.

"Market's down there, Aussie." His accent drew the world out until it sounded more like *ass-ey*.

I shook my head and raised a hand. "Thanks."

"Plaza is three blocks that way. Just turn right, and right again." A different bum, wrapped in three coats and stuffed with newspapers, pointed out hopefully.

"Thanks, mate."

I scraped my fingers to the bottom of my Santa hat, pulling out the couple of bucks and whatever coinage had been donated to Pickles' spitty cause, and held it out to him. "Merry Christmas."

The bum's eyes lit up, and he reached out. A slim hand intercepted me.

"Nope. Not that one. Moving right along." A flash of tinsel lit up my world as the same hand wrapped around my elbow, sliding between me and Pickles. Suddenly I was paraded across the intersection, surrounded by gaggle of chattering tourists, holding phones up for pictures and ogling maps, similar to how I had a moment before.

"Wait, I need–"

"Nope. Trust me, Aussie. You really don't *need* his charity."

I stared down at this tiny woman – elf – between us, dressed in striped tights, high black walking boots, the red nose, and reindeer face paint. A headband fixed with antlers made her tiny frame almost top Pickles at his full five-feet, eight-inches height, the tall bugger.

Her crowning achievement was the small string of flashing Christmas lights on the headband and wrapped around her head in a multicoloured, glowing halo.

Deep brown eyes twinkled beneath thick curled lashes. She stared up at me with a saucy grin on her face. "Joey has a house down the block. Big one. Don't give Christmas cheer to those who don't deserve it. He probably earns more than I do." She grimaced.

I blinked as my feet hit the pavement at the other side of the intersection, chancing a glance over my shoulder where Joey accosted someone else, one shoulder dropped and forming a limp he hadn't had a moment before.

"He's a fake?"

She nodded. "We've got a few of them. Regulars. But Joey is known to basically everyone locally. Only the new business owners tend to feed him, and any cash goes straight to extra Christmas cheer." She waggled her eyebrows. "Why are you in New York, and why aren't you on my tour? Doesn't he look lost?" She asked her tour group, who wrapped around us in a tight circle.

Pickles honked his alarm and backed up a few paces as hands descended on him.

Definitely not my best idea.

"I am lost. The– Joey was pointing in the direction of the Plaza Hotel."

"That's where you're staying?" She covered a snort, her eyes twinkling at me in a way that left blood rushing from my head. "They aren't gonna like the alpaca."

"This boy is a living legend," I reached across her shoulders and gave Pickles a pat on the back of his neck, twisting his halter in my fingers. He gave me another sideways glance, fixing his gaze on the glowing thing between us. "Behave," I muttered.

He gave me a wounded look and nuzzled the Santa hat he tried to eat earlier in the day.

"Are you talking to me or to him?" The girl between us laughed softly, rubbing Pickles, then wrapped an arm around both of us, pulling us together in a three person hug. "Smile!"

"What? Gah," I growled, emulating Pickles' best honk as a flash when off in my face, obliterating my vision. Pickles reared back, almost head-butting me. "The hell was that?" I swiped a hand in front of my eyes, but my vision was covered in snowy dots.

"Barry likes to make coffee table books. Don't you, Barry?" she yelled at the man who popped out from around his camera. "What's your name?" she asked me in an undertone.

"Ford."

"Nisha." She rocked between me and the alpaca. "Barry, this is Ford."

The short, balding man who looked more like the Godfather than a coffee table book maker, touched his ear where a small device sat and answered the question before the one she just asked. "Yes, ma'am."

I blinked, trying to catch up. "How many people can you talk to at once?"

A gaggle of tourists on an opposing tour darted at us from the other direction. Nisha waved, yelling something out another woman replied to before herding her crowd in the opposite direction. She lurched across me to grab Barry's arm as the photo vendor teetered sideways against the influx of pedestrian traffic. A quick glance at ground level showed the man wore a prosthetic.

I scrambled for change in my Santa hat. "How much?"

The man rattled off his prices as I extracted a twenty from the depths of the reed velvet. I pushed all the change into his hand, shaking my head when he tried to take the coins only.

"Merry Christmas."

He scribbled a name on a card along with an email address and grinned broadly. "I remember the alpaca."

I smiled. "Probably."

"Thanks, Barry. See you tomorrow." The effervescent Nisha pushed me onward, talking over her shoulder in a tour guide voice to the gaggle at her back, dragging us all along like so many obedient workshop elves.

"–a better use of your money?" She aimed at me, pausing to draw breath, and then threw the next line of her tour over her shoulder.

"As long as it gets me to the Plaza Hotel, sure." I rubbed the back of my neck, bemused as Chriatmas chaos whirled around me in a frenzied glow of Christmas lights and reindeer face paint.

"We'll get you there."

She nodded, her glowing antlers bobbing and emitting a soft Christmas carol I couldn't quite put my finger on. She continued to drag Pickles and I across what felt like half of New York City, pointing out various landmarks and yelling in a bright voice the entire street could hear. Probably the next few blocks.

My ears were ringing by the time we navigated across the next intersection, and she pointed out the Plaza Hotel on my left where a branded, stoic doorman waited, his hands held stiffly and his sides like a giant nutcracker.

"And your final destination is right there. What are you in town for again?" She collected cash from each of the tourists as her tour ended.

Shadows lengthened around us while I picked out landmarks on the opposing corners so I wouldn't get lost again.

"Uh, thanks," I started as a gray-headed granny pushed her way through to Nisha, wrapping her arm around the tiny woman's neck and embracing her until all I could see was the glowing tips of her antlers.

In a flurry of *thank yous* and *goodbyes*, the tour group departed in their separate directions, more than one bundling their arms around themselves as they walked. Pickles, the traitor, snuggled up to my tour guide while she snapped selfies with him without getting spat on.

Will miracles never cease?

Then her attention turned on me, and I lost focus on everything else. Those liquid brown stared up at me and paired with that soft pink mouth spread in a wide smile, everything around me sparkled like Christmas morning.

"I'm in town for a wedding."

"Oh, I know the one." Nisha nodded as though she knew the details of every wedding in NYC.

She probably does.

"Ah, good then." I stood awkwardly, avoiding passers by. "Can I have my alpaca back now, please?" I asked politely.

"He's needy, isn't he?" Nisha murmured to Pickles, rubbing his nose affectionately. He let her feed him and coo all over him.

"I'm not the needy one," I grumbled.

"And grumpy, too."

I huffed and didn't object to that. "So, thank you for helping me find my hotel."

I wasn't sure if I wanted the girl to disappear or ask her to come up and help me find my room.

What the hell is wrong with me?

I never let people into my personal space. Ever. Even if they were cute as all get out and dressed like a reindeer-elf hybrid.

"I'm gonna give you a tour of New York," Nisha announced. "I'll even waive my fees 'til Christmas. I get the feeling you don't love it here and I can't let you go back to wherever you came from without falling in love."

Her eyes glowed, and it wasn't the city that held my attention.

"Uh, sure," I replied dumbly.

"Great!" She slipped a card into my hand. "Right here, nine am. I'll pick you up tomorrow."

"Thanks." I took the card with her number and a happy little Santa hat next to her name. "Nisha Lister. You might have just saved my Christmas." I offered her a bemused smile.

"If you get that alpaca into the Plaza, I'll eat that Santa hat before Pickles does." She grinned at me again. "And I'll see you tomorrow at nine. Morning time, no sleep ins."

"Not a night owl, huh?" I closed my hand into a fist, counting the hours I needed to make up for work while I wandered lost around the city.

"Early bird gets the tourists," she called, and waved at me over the shoulder.

Her hips swayed temptingly side to side as she walked away, still full of more energy than most people I knew.

My lost day had turned into a semi-productive day, and at least I found my accommodation. Baring my teeth and praying money spoke more than a smile, I led Pickles toward the doorman who stared in horror at my camelid, and then at me.

"You've got to be joking," he muttered, not reaching for the door.

Pickles chose that moment to defecate tiny pellets in a neat little pyramid right on the hotel's front doorstep.

I gave the doorman a broad grin, gritted my teeth, and reached for the door myself.

"Nope. Merry Christmas."

CHAPTER 2

NISHA

"GOTTA GET A BETTER JACKET THAN THAT," Jeramiah Wallace, the super at my building and local elderly who loved to perch on the doorstep and people watch, commented as I climbed the steps with weary feet. "Snow's coming on. I feel it in my knees."

Jeremiah had been predicting a white out Christmas with his knees for the last five years straight, and we hadn't gotten one yet.

"Not going to happen this year, Mister Wallace," I muttered, digging for my keys in my purse. My antlers fell over my face, obscuring everything. "Fuck."

"Language, Miss Lister," Jeremiah reproached me. "You won't go about finding a nice young man with a mouth like that."

"Oh, you love it," I sassed him for the hell of it. "Do you need any groceries, or anything taken up?" I stopped beside the little old man who could barely fix a tap.

Our building fell down around us and our twenty-three tenants, of whom I knew a good dozen by first name. The others were little more than night shift ghosts, especially over the silly season.

"I can look after myself." Jerry sat proudly. Something cracked in his back and he winced. "Mostly."

I grinned. "I'm going to knock on your door at the first snowflake tomorrow, and you're going to give me any of your prescriptions you want topped up, plus a list of what you need for Christmas. Are we doing our regular breakfast, or lunch this year?"

"Are you making that nice ham again?" The super tried to sound disinterested, but his sneaky side glance gave him away.

"Of course I am."

"Make sure you get those fancy cherries for the top then." Jerry sank back to his slouch on the stoop, returning to watching the stragglers slosh past in the melting mud that covered the pavement.

"Will do."

Resisting the urge to pat his balding dome, I lugged my own groceries onto my hip and traipsed up the stairs humming about Jeremiah the Bullfrog. Finally locating my key in my fanny pack, I used the last of my energy to reach my scarred door that barely hung on its worn hinges, and stepped inside my apartment. Breath left me in a whoosh, the day's conversations still whirling around my head in fragments and echoes. I closed my eyes, leaning back on the door.

One day I'll have quiet.

But for now, the tours were my lifeline to pay rent, eat, and exist.

And I offered Mister Alpaca Man three days' free work at my busiest, most lucrative tip time of the year.

What the hell is wrong with me?

He was cute, but not that cute. Okay, so maybe he was that cute. And I wasn't talking about that alpaca. Though the fuzzy beast had a certain appeal.

Groaning, I pushed off the door that seemed to hold a whole lot more gravity than before and began to unpack my groceries, counting the moments before I could shower beneath my rusty faucet, praying there was enough hot water left, and sleep before my alarm went off far too early the next morning. Maybe work out what Ford No-last-name-yet needed to know about New York for the few days he was in town and show him what tourists only missed.

Maybe dream about him a little as well.

That secret little smile while he wasn't bantering back with me, the light behind his eyes while I kissed him and soothed his inner beast. That brought up images of the alpaca rocking an underbite, and I giggled.

Because any fantasy was better than the lonely Christmas in the apartment block where we all pretended we had family who cared and ended up creating one with those around us instead.

Another lonely Christmas.

I pushed the thought aside, kicking off my elf boots without untying them and pushed the all too sexy Ford and his cute alpaca from my mind.

Unsuccessfully.

I STOOD outside the Plaza covered in a light snow that dusted me head to toe, holding an alpaca harness while Ford figured out currency.

"I promised I wouldn't be caught without change after yesterday," he muttered, flicking notes over and peering at them

"This isn't how I saw today going either," I assured Pickles, who grunted softly and shuffled around me, inhaling the pom poms on my dress. "Don't you eat my elf suit."

"He might take a nibble," Ford admitted. "I think he misses sharpening his teeth on the gum trees at home."

I shot him a look at the apparently constantly ravenous alpaca who nuzzled me. "They do that?"

"Nope," Ford said cheerfully, finally figuring his tips out and handing me a wad of cash while he stuffed everything else–including his passport–into his back pocket. "Here."

"You're gonna get robbed," I sighed, flapping two free fingers on the hand holding Pickles' halter. "Give it over. I'll zip it up."

"Thanks." Ford ignored my fingers, unzipping my pouch and stuffing his passport and the wad of cash he retrieved from my other hand inside. "Appreciate it."

"Whoa, I'm not your camel," I protested. "Nor am I your maid. I'm not carrying your cash." My idea of taking Ford touring fast lost its glitter, but those deep blue eyes still held my attention.

Ford grinned at me. "I'm not letting you work for free at Christmas, Nisha."

"Huh?" I blinked owlishly at him. "Wha– no. Nope," I repeated firmly. "That's way too much."

"No take backs." Ford wound his hand around the halter rein, his knuckles grazing my hand as he tried to relieve me of my burden. "Uh, can I have my alpaca back now please?" he asked, grinning impishly.

My eyes narrowed, and I tried to ignore the sparks that lit my skin like a Christmas tree wherever he touched me. "You aren't half the bumpkin you pretended to be yesterday, are you?" I accused him.

"Me?" His eyes sprang open wide. "I would never."

I snorted. "Bullshit." Too late I remembered Jeremiah's

comment about dating and nice men and foul mouths...but on second reflection, Ford didn't seem to care.

He shook his head, laughing at me. "Damn, girl. You're good value."

"You live here." I put my hands on my hips, determined to get the truth he wasn't telling me out into the open between us.

Ford pointed to himself. "Aussie. Accent." He laid on the slang thick enough to butter a vegemite sandwich, though his gaze shifted, a slight tint of pink reddening his nose.

I waggled a finger in his face. "Rubbish. Then you have lived here before."

He shrugged easily. "You got me. I'm in town for Rex and Chelsea's wedding. I roomed with Rex at Columbia for a year at college."

"Oh." I started walking. Pickles followed me, honking softly and dragging his owner along with him. "What did you study?"

"Economics, and law."

I stopped. "You're a lawyer?"

"I'm a business owner," he said with the slightest hesitation. "I run alpacas and a few other things from Western Australia, though I travel a bit. Usually unaccompanied." He gave Pickles a pointed look.

"Mhmm." I made a disgruntled noise. Pickles honked his approval. "Thank you." I ruffled his fluff and fixed his bucket, leaning in confidentially. "I think he's full of it too. Where do you want to go?"

Pickles turned a corner. I talked as we walked with the alpaca in the lead—why not, after all?—pointing out the Rockefeller Centre, The William Tecumseh Monument and Tiffany & Co., in case he had a special someone to buy for.

"Do you?" I asked idly, when he stopped and stared in the window.

Ford flashed me a grin. "Never have time to stop for that long." He lingered a moment longer, staring at the reflection of a huge skyscraper recently built behind us. Its green and gold tinted windows flashed in the glare from the clouds above as it finally stopped snowing lightly.

Sunlight shone through the clouds in a *hallelujah* moment.

"The FCMC building?" I wrinkled my nose as Ford turned on his heel to stare up at the behemoth. "Recently built. The dust and pollution was horrendous, though it went up fast. A security firm for celebrities, apparently, a whole plethora of law firms and the owner has a portfolio that seems to cover half the globe, or so I've heard. The bottom floors are rented out to local businesses. Rumors also say the penthouse bathrooms are gilt in gold and silver with green marble," I gossiped readily, walking on to avoid Ford's intense stare as his gaze shifted to me, pinning me where I stood, slightly more breathless than before. "Purchased by some foreign party, apparently. I haven't looked into who, but I can, if you're interested. Though I also heard there was a calamity of some sort and it was up for sale. Do I have a snowflake on my nose or something?" I chattered on for a moment then stared at him, my hands on my hips.

Pickles stopped, too, looking curiously at Ford.

"No, you're cute as a button." His gaze softened as he looked at me. "Keep up that whirlwind attitude. It's refreshing. I need more of that."

I tilted my head to one side, resuming my tour with a quick rundown of the other businesses around us including the Apple building if only to break the tension wrapped around him. Ford had a hard side, maybe the business ethic that allowed him to stuff several thousand dollars at a girl he didn't know, and bribe the formidable Plaza to allow his alpaca inside.

"What, they don't move fast where you're from?" I teased lightly.

"Hell, no." Ford let out a laugh that did fun things to my insides.

He's just a job.

"So, slow and sleepy and...country bumpkin?"

Pickles hummed and turned another corner.

"Yup, that's me. All the slow things." Ford tugged on Pickles' lead. "Who's holding this tour anyway, buddy?"

"Why do you have an alpaca in tow?" He looked so lost the day before, I just kind of went with it. NYC was like that. Lots of people who looked like they never stopped or slept, but it wasn't them who were standing still.

"He's meant to be finding a lady friend, but she wasn't available and I couldn't reach the owners I arranged to meet up with upstate. I've got another five boys on loan out for stud in Cali to collect on my way home, but they can stay for a few months to get the job done if necessary. Or we can freeze the goods and they can be used at will."

"That's not very romantic, is it?" I scratched Pickles' ears. "We'll get you a date, big guy. Got any talents?"

"He sings," Ford muttered under his breath, snorting when I glanced at him with two eyebrows raised. "When he approaches a female he sort of hums and grunts, even if he's a good twenty feet away, like getting in the mood. When he stops, about twenty minutes later, the deed is done. My nephew from Sydney calls it, "Pickles' happy song."

"Beautiful. You know I'm going to use that anecdote sometime on a tour."

"Go go right ahead. I have zero shame."

I grin. "What happened to reduce that?"

Ford didn't answer, reading a shop sign. "I think this is where I have to pick up my suit later. For the wedding."

"Ahh, the wedding. We've all heard about it," I sighed

dramatically. "There have been suppliers running ragged to get things to the Plaza all December. If you listen to that sort of gossip."

"And you do."

"I do. Kind of my bread and butter to know who is doing what. Tourists love that sort of stuff. What do you like, though?" I asked, keen to tailor his NYC experience since his alpaca seemed so cute.

Also, his owner.

Stop that.

I swore my head was in the clouds as I took note of the shop name. "When do you need to collect your suit?"

"This afternoon at four."

I rearranged the map in my head so we would finish at the right time on the correct side of the street for him. "Okay, we can do that."

"The rehearsal dinner is tonight. And a few old friends want to head out after." He grimaced.

Socializing wasn't his thing? He came across as easy going, but hey, I met the man all of a day ago. "You're not a fan?" I frowned. "Aren't you celebrating with your friend?"

"Let's just say I have a history of shitty pre-wedding arrangements. I might not be very talkative tomorrow," he admitted. "Fair warning. Plus the wedding is in the afternoon.."

I walked a block in silence, turning his words over in my head. "Is that why you aren't keen to do all the socializing and jazz, spending your days with me so easily instead?"

"Nah, you bullied me into it." His quick grin was back, though his gaze lingered on my face for a moment before he took in the city buzzing around him. "Is it antlers all December for you?" He patted Pickle's santa hat, his odd mood dispelled.

"Did not," I answered his first question and led them

through a small arcade. "And it's antlers from November, thank you very much. As soon as my witch costume comes off for Halloween. Let me show you some of the city's best kept secrets."

SIX HOURS LATER, my feet ached in the best of ways and Pickles walked slowly at my side. Ford's bright eyes and bushy tail never wavered, pushing on with a sense of curiosity and wonder of the city brought together by tinsel and Christmas lights.

The snow probably helped.

"It doesn't get like this in Australia, does it?" I crinkled my nose trying to remember, and came up with an image of a big red rock and blue skies. Maybe some surfer dudes that looked like they were cast in *Point Break.*

"Not usually. There's a few places where it gets cold, but that's about all. Certainly none out my way."

"Glad you get to experience this then." I smiled as he turned around on his heel, staring up at the buildings towering over us. "This is where you need to pick up your suit, right? I'll get Pickles."

"Appreciate it." Ford poked his head inside, the door shutting behind him. He reappeared a few minutes later while I was planning out tomorrow's shortened trip and failing. "Nisha? Can I get an opinion please?"

His manner was formal and reserved, so different from the easygoing alpaca farmer for whom nothing seemed to be a burden apart from weddings.

"Sure." I tugged on Pickles' lead but he resisted. "Come on, buddy," I used Ford's term of endearment, but the caramel-colored alpaca was having none of it. "Come *on.*"

"Dude." Ford leaned out of the shop, grabbed the halter, and tugged.

The alpaca tugged too, but not moving Ford. He retreated a few steps, pulling Ford out of the shop.

"This isn't a good idea–" I started.

Pickles beat me to it. He sat suddenly, lurching downward in the middle of the sidewalk camel style in a puddle of slush kicked up by passing traffic and passersby.

I groaned at the sight. "The Plaza isn't going to like that." I still wasn't sure how much Ford paid to get the alpaca into the hotel, but the bribe must have been substantial. Mind, he threw a wad of cash into my pack earlier, and though I hadn't counted it, I knew those dollars would pay my rent and groceries for well over two months.

All because he doesn't want to socialize?

I wrinkled my nose. There had to be more to it than that.

Turning to calm both the annoyed alpaca owner and the beast itself–or the other way around–I put out a hand, stepping into Ford. "Maybe you should give him some space. What do you need?"

"I need–"

I never got to find out what Ford needed because Pickles chose that moment to throw a toddler tantrum, tossing his head back as far as a three foot neck can go.

Ford tumbled out of the shop door, his socked feet peddling on ice and landed face first in a pile of slush beside pickles.

"Fuck," he muttered, levering himself out of the muck.

I covered my mouth with one hand to conceal the snort of laughter that threatened, and patted the alpaca's back. "There, are you okay now?"

Ford shot me a dirty look. "Thanks," he said dryly.

"You're welcome. What did you want?" I twisted in my crouch

to stare up at him as he stood. His front was completely covered in slush and muck, but his unbuttoned shirt clung to his body and displayed a slice of ripped abs decorated with tendrils of ink.

My mouth hung open. "Oh, wow."

"That bad?" He winced, tugging at the saturated material. "I'll go in and…fix this, Somehow. The legs are too short right?"

"Huh?" I was still staring at his midsection and may have drooled on his alpaca.

"Nisha. Eyes up here," Ford said softly.

My cheeks heated until my face glowed like a Christmas bauble. I blinked at him. "Oh. Cuffs. Right. Yes, they could use a little length," I whispered.

"Noted." He nodded briskly, but his eyes remained on my face as he turned, and disappeared into the shop while I crouched beside his filthy alpaca and thought dirty thoughts.

CHAPTER 3

FORD

COMING BACK to New York City was a calamity. I towel dried Pickles from his bath–thank God for whoever invented shower hoses–and led him cautiously off the tiles to his corner of the room where his newspaper was spread over a square three feet. Fortunately alpacas tended to keep their poop in a pile, else convincing the staff downstairs and letting them hold one of my credit cards on file would have been a whole lot harder.

Pickle's head disappeared into his freshly filled bucket and he snuffled away at the feed, his honks echoing from the inside of the red plastic.

"At least you're clean." I shucked the ruined shirt from my shoulders and tossed it into the bathroom. Mud splattered everywhere, and I knew I'd have to leave a hell of a tip for the poor cleaner in the morning.

A hot shower washed away the muck I fell into. There was no hiding the horror on the tailor's face when I walked back into his shop wearing the street's mud on my front, but thankfully he had enough stock to fix the problem–and my slacks' cuffs.

Nisha promised to collect the items for me as soon as they were ready, barely holding in her giggles as she delivered us back to the front of the Plaza Hotel.

I tipped the doorman discreetly, giving Nisha a quick wave, though I couldn't tear my gaze from her face as she chatted cheerily with the hotel staff as Pickles led me inelegantly through the turnstile doors, dripping all over the freshly cleaned carpet in the foyer.

I followed his lead, wondering if Nisha was always so friendly with everyone. The girl seemed to have a bottomless pit of cheer ready on hand, but I couldn't shake the memory of the way she looked at me with my filthy, open shirt plastered to my body.

Avoiding the pre-wedding prep with an excuse of jet lag though I arrived weeks earlier for my stud tour with my boy tribe of alpacas seemed like a great idea. Right up until I realised how much of a hell spending days with the cute, quirky and whirlwind of a girl would be.

Because *cute as a button* didn't come close to covering the flush of heat that deluged me whenever I swept my gaze over Nisha's dark hair tucked into her beanie, or the reflected Christmas lights dancing in her eyes.

Or how my body reacted to that look she gave me when her gaze ran up my snow-mucked torso.

Part of me wanted to count down the days til I could say goodbye.

The other half wanted to find out how she spent her Christmas, and if she wanted to come halfway across the globe to find out how I spent mine.

CHAPTER 4

NISHA

THE SECOND DAY I waited outside the Plaza Hotel for Ford, the sun shone down brightly, nary a snowflake in sight. The streets were busy with shoppers and more suppliers and decorators who delved into the bowels of the Plaza in preparation for the wedding.

And for the first time, he was late.

Not that I had much of a benchmark, but he was adamant on being on time to collect his suit–the calamity that closed off our first full day together–and he was waiting for me bright and early the day before. Today seemed....out of character.

I checked my watch at ten to ten. Breaking my own rules, I waved to the doorman–Samuel, I checked–on my way into the Plaza Hotel. I never asked for guests at the desk. It didn't matter if they needed a sleep in, were in coitus or had some form of emergency.

No one liked being poked. And they could join the tour, if they wanted, the next day.

But Ford... He was different.

I waited in line and approached the desk, poking my head around the small divider. "Can I have a tour prompt call to Ford, please?" I smiled. When she gave me a blank face, I grinned. "The guy with the Aussie accent and the alpaca."

"Oh my gosh. You mean Ford Millham." She made a swooning gesture, and picked up the phone tapping in a number she knew by heart.

My gaze narrowed.

"What –"

"Yes, your ten o'clock?" She risked a glance at me, eyebrows rising.

"Nine," I mouthed back.

She grimaced. "Your tour guide is at the desk." She grinned and gave me a thumbs up.

I shrugged as she hung up. "Whatever works."

"Did you see him yesterday? Seriously swoon-worthy manflesh."

I sorted. "Yeah, I was there when he hit the slush."

She shook her head vehemently. "No, last night. I was on the late shift. I finish in half an hour. He came in after the party, fairly drunk and wearing– well. Not a lot." Her eyes glittered and her eyebrows waggled.

Oh hell. The rehearsal dinner, and the drinks or whatever afterward. I forgot.

"No wonder he's late." Then my curiosity got the better of me. "How little clothing?"

"Like, one thing. An ugly sweater and a sock on his–" Her cheeks blazed santa suit red.

"Cock." Ford's baritone voice boomed across the broad bottom floor of the Plaza Hotel.

"That thing is a weapon," I muttered, refusing to hang my head as every eye turned to focus on the tall Aussie.

Ford's voice might have it all going on, but the rest of him seemed...wilted. Dark circles hung under his eyes. Reddened flesh overlaid by fresh ink peeked out from the top of his black, tight t-shirt.

Dressed in jeans and cowboy boots, he looked ready to rumble.

In a cage fight, maybe.

Or the docks.

"What the hell happened to him?" I hissed over my shoulder at the drooling receptionist.

But seeing as Ford already shouted the word *'cock'* pretty much to the entire ground floor, there really weren't any eyes *not* fixed on the alpaca farmer.

"The cowboy and the elfling," Ford answered my question. I hadn't aimed at him.

"It is weapons-grade." The receptionist fanned herself shamelessly, still several steps back in the conversation.

Ford's cheeks tinted pink.

"If you say so. Come on. We have a boat to catch. Wait. Where's Pickles?"

"Sleeping off a hangover."

"You sure that's not you?"

"Pretty darn sure, elf girl." His voice still didn't match up to the story his face told, and there was no way I wasn't asking what he got tattooed on his chest overnight.

We are halfway along the block before I mention my first question, glancing between him and the harassed looking Christmas shoppers. "So – how did the par–?"

"Finish that sentence, and you'll never cuddle Pickles ever again," Ford threatened.

"Ouch. That's just nasty. Are you sure I can't ask–"

"What happens after the rehearsal dinner stays at the—well. Wherever we went," Ford closed the subject off firmly.

I exhaled through my nose, and made a decision that could lose me my cute client. Without taking another breath, I rose on my toes, grabbed the collar of his tee, and took a quick peek inside.

A familiar snout and ears stared back at me with a spectacular underbite beneath his Santa hat. Laughter lodged in my throat that ended in a coughing fit as my eyes welled.

"Tell me Pickles has your face tattooed on his rump." I struggled to catch my breath, doubled over as the giggles escaped me. Tears followed, coursing down my cheeks as I howled on the sidewalk.

"Really? That's professional?" Ford grumped, but the hint of a smile curled the corner of his mouth.

"I'm wearing an elf costume. Several that I have in my closet with a fresh one each day for the twenty-four days of Christmas. How much more professional would you like, Ford?" I sassed him back. "Besides, I had to drag you out of bed. And you didn't bring your cute alpaca."

"Not the point." His tone shifted.

I twisted around, walking backward along the sidewalk. "Not the point?" I asked incredulously. "I waited for an hour, Ford. That's one good hangover."

"I have no idea what you're talking about."

Huffing, I led the way to the small private dock I booked out for the season, waving to the older gent with his small ferry waiting for us. "Probably a good thing. They wouldn't let Pickles on board."

"Maybe. I have my ways." Ford gave me a smile that left the solid ground wobbling beneath me, and I hadn't even gotten on the boat yet.

Putting on my best tour guide smile, I waved to the dock staff I recognised but the moment I put a foot out, Ford stepped up beside me. His hand outstretched, the hooded look that made it past his exhaustion giving me pause. Calluses covered his hand, and small scars.

Not an accountant's hand. Or a lawyer, or whatever else he tried to sell me.

I took the offer, though my balance was fine. My fingers closed around his rougher one, sensitive to the small jolts of pleasure and warmth at the contact.

The short gangplank shifted beneath me and I knew I made a misstep. For the first time in my life because that damned boat never gave me grief, and I got on it twice a day, every freaking day. Somehow my foot went over the side of the sturdy plank, and I started to fall.

Hard hands caught me before I dropped so much as an inch. Ford's mouth moved, but nothing made it through to me as I blinked up, and up at him.

Sweet baby Jesus, he's tall.

His abs were a wall of muscle that supported us both, his hand huge where it wound around my waist. Breath left me as he pulled me into his body and onto the boat in one step together.

Twisting my fingers into his shirt, I tried to suck in air, but his proximity snuffed out the oxygen in my lungs. I opted to concentrate on his face, making the mistake of holding his gaze. Heat smouldered there, contrasting sharply to the cheeky, killer smile on his arched lips.

"You with me, Nisha?" He hooked his arm around my waist, refusing to let me go as I tried to back pedal. "I need to know you're okay before I let you down."

I blinked at where my hands bunched at his shirt, and released him immediately, trying to take the promised step back.

The steel band at my back prevented any movement.

"Ford?" I tried again, heat rising in my cheeks.

He stared down at me a moment longer, rubbing circles over my lower back with firm fingers. "She's fine," he talked over my head. One hand slid down to squeeze my hip, the small boat rocking to draw us closer.

My eyes popped open in full as I realised the heat in his eyes wasn't limited to only one body part. I could feel it. Him, rather. I could feel him pressed against my stomach.

The receptionist hadn't lied.

Ford Millham's manflesh was indeed swoonworthy.

Enough to hang my Santa hat on.

I pushed away from him, and this time, he let me, giving me just enough space to find my seat near the ferryman and faced the front, pretending the supernova level glow in my cheeks was all about the chillfactor.

Not the manflesh that had the ability to melt polar ice caps seated several feet behind me.

"Good weather today, Miss Nisha," Jansen called as he steered his boat-cum-ferry in the interest of bolstering his non-existent pension away from the peer. "Standard loop?"

"Make it longer," I muttered, fixing my gaze on a building upriver.

My regular spiel sat on my tongue, but for the life of me I couldn't bring the words any further to Ford. Jansen hummed a mangled Christmas carol I didn't bother to untangle while I ignored my passenger and tried to get my Christmas baubles together.

Sure, Ford pinned me. I was a whirlwind mess most of the time, but I managed a business, and paid my bills on time, even if I didn't get to save much each week. Plus, there were a few structured people in my life–Jeremiah (the bullfrog) Superintendent I'd have Christmas lunch with–I made a hasty note on the back of my hand to pick up the ham I ordered for us plus cherries or he'd never forgive me when I ran us out of hot water on cold nights ever again.

And Jansen, my trusty ferryman. We'd never lost a passenger or a parcel between us. I counted that as a win. Denise, the other half of the tour pair we made, divvying up customers and booking out small events together.

And...Ford.

I cleared my throat, ready to point out Lady Liberty and the Christmas decorations that hugged NYC like an elf suit of its own, some so large they were visible from the water.

Anything to distract myself from the six foot four cowboy infatuation behind me.

Ford sat quietly a few rows back, the lone passenger on a private tour. I couldn't face him for the first ten minutes, but when I managed to sneak a glance over my shoulder as the boat turned smoothly, he rested his arms across the seat backs either side of him, head tilted back, taking in the view and the fresh air.

Some of his dark mood from before dropped away, and I steeled myself enough to approach him.

"I'm sorry about before," I murmured as I worked my way between the seats to perch at the edge of his row.

Ford turned his head, spotting where I sat, and crooked one finger on his outstretched arm. "Closer."

Wild reindeer fidgeted in my stomach.

I closed my hands on the plastic seats, berating myself for giving into his flirtatious nature, and scooted two seats over, leaving one square foot of plastic as neutral ground.

"Closer."

When I hesitated, Ford's fingers curled gently around my shoulder and tugged me into the spare seat between us.

Okay, so I moved into the spare seat between us. But his hand was most definitely my scapegoat.

His gaze swept over me, from my elf shoes to my antlers, and settled on my face. "You're not a reindeer today."

I pressed a hand to my cheek, frowning. "I forgot." Then I

elbowed him. "I was rushing to get Jeramiah's meds *and* meet you and you were damn well late, Ford." I poked him for good measure and almost broke a finger. "Ow."

"I think I'm the one who's meant to say that."

"You'd deserve it," I grumbled.

"That upset I touched you, huh?" He squeezed the shoulder he hadn't released in an intimate gesture I shouldn't have let pass, but I did.

It was cold.

My argument was shitty. Or spitty, depending if you asked Pickles or not.

"I don't usually um, you know..." I squeezed my eyes shut and blew out a breath.

"Flirt?"

"Yeah." I cracked one eye open. "Is it that bad?"

"Fairly crappy, but I'm sure you'll improve."

"Thanks."

"*Oof.*" Ford wheezed as I poked him a little harder this time. "Damn, girl."

"So, let's rephrase. I'm that bad at flirting, huh?" I pressed a fingertip to my chin and pretended to think.

"You're doing fabulous," Ford said with a straight face, sneaking a look at me out of the corner of my eye. He grabbed my free hand in his and raised it to his lips.

Warmth spread through my hands to my arms, every nerve ending pinging.

"What was that for?" I squeaked in a hushed voice but there was no way Jansen would hear us over the boat's motor and the wind rushing in the opposite direction.

"Because you're beautiful and I get the feeling no one tells you."

"Oh."

Ford settled back, hugging me a little closer, a satisfied

smirk decorating his face. "So, I have to be back by one to get suited up."

"Suit's all organised. I was picking it up at midday." I slid a peek at him through my lashes. "How long are you staying in New York, Ford?"

"Dunno." He flexed his fingers in his lap, rubbing the pad of his thumb across a collection of white scars on his knuckles. "I was going to bug out at Christmas, or New Years, if something came up..." His gaze lifted to my face. "Something to keep me here a while longer."

My heart stopped, and didn't restart. "Ford?"

He raised his hand, the one covered in scars, and cupped my cheek gently. "Give me a reason to stay, Nisha."

I blinked at him, wishing something–anything–would eject from my brain, but that seemed to have taken an impromptu hiatus along with my heart. "I can't–" was what actually fell out of my mouth.

Ford's hand on my shoulder flexed and fell away. "Okay."

My heart plummeted with his touch, and I shifted back to my original seat, wrapping my arms around myself, but no amount of body warmth kept out the cold void filled with Christmas wishes and a sense of longing.

CHAPTER 5

FORD

THIS IS INSANE.

I met the girl two days ago, and I was begging her to settle in for a Christmas fling instead of heading home like I always planned?

What the hell is wrong with me?

No wonder Nisha stared at me like I was a psycho when I came onto her so damn strong.

She chanced a look at me—just like the one she shot me before I wrapped my arm around her and forced her into my side—and opened her mouth.

And her tour guide persona appeared.

For the next hour I listened to her regale me with all the reasons why New York was incredible—and she has some seriously good facts stored in there—and why tourists needed to stay a few extra days to discover all there was to offer.

What I wanted to discover was *her.*

But the way she skittered from me…hell, maybe I was that desperate.

Especially at this time of year.

With a wedding looming.

In literally hours. I wasn't doing the groomsman thing the way Rex planned, and last night turned out to be less an afterparty and more a few guys hanging out together, not all from the bridal party, getting hammered over broken hearts and lost loves while the groom was conspicuously absent.

And how I ended up with Pickles' visage tattooed to my pecs.

I let Nisha ramble on until the boat turned, and ballsed up. "I didn't go out last night with the wedding crew. At least, that's not what it turned out to be. I don't do the wedding thing because I got jilted. On my buck's night. By a stripper. Exactly…" I checked my watch, "three hundred and sixty-four days and ten hours ago."

Her mouth fell open. "Oh, Ford."

"Yeah. Pity on me, right? So here I am, running from my friends' wedding capers. And I'm supposed to have a date. You wanna throw off this tour thing, spend the afternoon in the spa at the Plaza and come with me?" I looked out over the water, unable to bear the sympathy swimming in her liquid gold eyes.

"Ford, I think you need to stop–" she started, scooting back to where I put her before I fucked this whole thing up the first time around.

"No," I said harshly, enough that Jansen turned in his driver's seat. Nisha waved him down. "I don't want to *stop and think*, Neesh. All I want is to have a date on my arm I can cling to when it gets rough tonight, and think how damn gorgeous she is in a dress I buy her. You're not the only one with an empty life, honey."

She gaped at me, water cascading over her thick black lashes. "I can't do that."

"Sure you can. You say yes, I give Jansen a Christmas bonus so he can go home and cuddle his grandkids, and you and I go shipping. Then massage and pampering for you while I figure myself out."

"You know that's not what the deal was."

"I'm changing the deal."

She sat quiet for a moment. "Are you sure?"

"I'm sure."

"Too fast, Ford."

I grinned. "Nah, too fast is telling you I already booked you into the spa for this afternoon and bought the dress."

Her mouth hung open. "You didn't."

"I did." I turned to face her. "Say yes, Nisha."

She blinked at me and did the unthinkable.

"Yes."

———

I KEPT Nisha's hand wrapped around mine firmly as we entered the Plaza Hotel. Dressed as always in her cute little elf suit, she pushed all the right buttons on me– today's tights were pink and white candy striped with glitter. And without the face paint, I got to see a little more of who she was beneath the Christmas overload that suited her so perfectly.

Leading her lest she disappear on me, I stepped into the Plaza Hotel with my head swirling with the scent of cinnamon buns we picked on the way from the ferry, to her pomegranate and berry scent that lingered between us.

Today finally went like I planned.

Right up until I raised my gaze to the foyer desk across the large open space in time to connect with a pair of cold blue eyes I prayed I'd never see ever again.

Jess.

When I told Nisha the story of my ex, leaving me for the stripper on my own buck's party night, I didn't expect to come face-to-face with her any time soon, like I summoned the demoness by mentioning her name

Worse, the bulky, overspray tanned man she left me for lumbered at her side.

I halted midstride, and Nisha ran into me.

"What? Ford?" She peeked around me, scanning past the pair who lounged against the reception desk like they belonged there. "Did somebody let Pickles out?"

"He shouldn't be back from his appointment yet." I'd send him off to have his sperm frozen, so the trips to the US weren't as frequent.

"Oh."

I inhaled a long breath and walked on as thought I hadn't seen my ex, and she wasn't watching me like a cat got the cream, her greedy, icy gaze travelling over my body like I was something she wanted to lick.

A shudder worked its way through me, and I clutched Nisha tighter. Jess mouthed *upstairs,* and pointed a talon tipped nail towards the ceiling.

Her stripper friend grinned at me.

Blowing out the breath that was meant to offer a slice of sanity in a chaotic world, I turned to face Nisha. "Listen, the massage place is on the top floor. You'll need this key." I scrounged in my pocket for the one I collected earlier from the receptionist at some ungodly hour wearing a knitted sock on my cock. "Why don't you go up? They're expecting you. Then come and find me. I'm in room 1779."

Nisha plucked the key from my fingers, peering at it speculatively. "This is some sort of joke, right? Like you're not actually asking me to be your real date and..."

I read the hesitancy in her tone and my chest grew heavy.

"No. It's not a joke." *Maybe I should stay in the US longer.* Maybe that was the joke, and I hadn't been privy to it til now.

Jess' blade of a voice cut through the silence that hung around us. "Oh, yes, I've known him for years. And the secrets I can tell you..."

I squeezed my eyes shut, and rubbed the back of my neck. "Fuck me."

"Ford?"

"You're going to wear my name out if you say that often," I said, my voice hard. I closed my eyes again and opened them to find her watching me cautiously. "Headache," I murmured. It wasn't a lie. Jess brought those on pretty effectively.

"Okay." Nisha slipped to hand from my grasp to claim the key. "Do I need a code for the lift?"

"Shit. You do." I rattled off the massage suite number that would give her access. "Room 1779. Find me after. Promise?" I released a hand and tipped her head back with my knuckle. My skin prickled with little shocks, and I barely held back the urge to make out with her right there in the foyer. Heedless of the warning bells in my mind where anything Jess oriented was concerned, I leaned Ford, brushing my mouth across the corner of Nisha's.

"Okay," she whispered uncertainty after a stalled breath from us both, lifting her deep brown eyes, and turned away to the lift, throwing a slightly bemused look over her shoulder back at me.

Then she was gone, leaving me to face New York City socialite menace I wish I never got involved with.

I used to live here.

I told Nisha I went to Columbia with Rex, but I hadn't told her everything. Not yet. After the wedding, maybe. If she still wanted anything to do with me then.

Weaving my way around trolleys delivering bunches of

flowers and silky fabrics, I made my way back to Jess and grabbed her elbow. "Right. Let's go."

"What about Matty?" she mewled, scratching at my arm in an attempt to pry my hand off her. Fortunately, my jacket offered some resistance until she started on my fingers.

"You know, there was a time when I would've given anything to have your hands on me, Jess. But right now, all I want to do is get you whatever you want to get you out of my life. Permanently. As in I never want to hear from you ever again." I held her gaze and spoke loud enough at the entire reception team to let out a collective gasp.

I didn't give a fuck.

Jess huffed and puffed curses all the way to the elevator bank on the opposite side of the foyer area. No way in hell was I putting her and Nisha in a small space together.

"She won't last two nights with you," Jess coated the evilly victorious words in venom.

I dropped my hand from her arm and prompted her into the lift. She grabbed the stripper, clutching his hand and dragged him inside with us.

"Keep your thoughts off Nisha," I snapped, the elevator car shrinking by the minute and taking all breathable air with it.

Then I winced.

"Nisha." Jess' smile widened, her scarlett lips matched to her talons. "I'll be sure to say hello at the reception later. She is your date for that, isn't she? Does she know?"

The doors closed and the lift began to move. I turned on her, slapping my hand into the mirror behind her head. "If you say a single fucking word, I swear–" I roared right in her face.

Jess had the decency to look terrified.

A large, meaty hand gripped my shoulder. "Not cool." Matty waggled a finger side to side in my face.

I stepped back, pushing my hair off my face. "Fuck."

"See now, she doesn't know what you're like, does she?" Jess cooed in a little singsong voice, sidling over to Matt, and rubbing her hands long is torso. "And I suit you much better. Just admit it." Her gaze turned speculative. "You know, the three of us could have fun."

Disgust rose from my stomach into my throat. "You did me a favour, you know."

Her eyes opened comically wide as she was getting something for her efforts.

"You left me, but you freed my time up to find somebody more."

Her wide eyes narrowed. "More *what?*"

"Anything, really," I said softly. "She's nothing like you, thank God."

She smiled viciously at me, shoving her way out of the elevator the moment the doors opened.

"I thought you wanted to talk," I said blandly, throwing on the business face I used with any regular asshole I came across, including my ex.

"With you?" She slapped my chest hard enough to sting.

I rocked back on my heels, sliding my hands into my pockets, and said nothing, knowing my lack of response would infuriate her. I'd given her enough of a reaction and I'd wear the consequences of that at some later point. Jess' venom knew no bounds.

"You're always like this!" she shrieked, hitting overdrive in seconds. "I can't talk to you, I can't get any sense out of you. You're impossible!"

I tilted my head to one side and held my silence.

Whatever she wanted, she washed out this round. I stepped out of the lift and headed towards my door, my key in my hand.

"Don't you ignore me! You're always so mean," Jess raged.

I had to laugh, turning it into a cough into my fist, angling a curious look sideways.

Matty leaned against the wall as he played on his phone, his face completely blank. Apparently he was as used to Jess' tantrums as me. I was surprised they lasted a year.

Happy Jilt Day to me.

Jess was still raging as I slipped my door open and held my foot in place, blocking the doorway, so she couldn't barge her way in.

"What do you want, Jess?" I managed calmly, regretting my anger from before, but none of that was left.

"Money," she hissed, and swiped up at me violently.

Cute, considering she was a foot shorter than me.

"I gave you five."

"Five minutes?" Matt looked up from his phone, confused.

"Five mil," Jess snapped at him, the figure rolling off her tongue like so much pocket change. "Wake up, Matty. Follow along like a big boy, now."

He mumbled something I didn't understand.

Jess turned her fury back at me. "That M better change to a B pretty fast, Ford."

I shot. "Or what, Jess? We went over this. Five mil was a fairly big payday for you, and for eight weeks of utter hell, you fleeced me. Congratulations. Why don't you go and stand on the corner with Matty?"

Regret and self loathing slammed me the moment that I let the vitriol affect me.

"Asshole," she said to my back.

I said nothing else, sliding out of the doorway, closing it softly.

No way in hell was Jess working her way back into my life. I wasn't over the last damage she did in a not so glorious eight weeks.

Eight weeks. The first few days were cute, until I realised

what a gold digger she was. Because I bought into the line she strung me along, wrapped in promises of family and christmases and forever sort of love. Then she dug nails in, and hadn't let go since.

Yanking out my phone I sent off a text to my lawyer, Richard.

Me: **Jess is back, be ready for whatever she throws at us.**

Richard: **Jesus, I'm booked until after Christmas, but you want to catch up while you're in town? I'm in the building.**

I knew he didn't mean the Plaza.

Me: **Let's see how it goes. I'm pretty packed. Maybe after Christmas.**

Richard: **Calendar's always open for you, man.**

RICHARD TOWNSEND WAS another Colombia buddy. He flew through law school, earning himself a partnership in one of the country's top law firms within five years. Now, he headed up my legal team. A natural force of his own, the lawyer focussed on business contracts and had nothing to do with marriage or relationships, but he researched for me and could write a prenup with the best of them.

The moment Jess read the terms, she was gone. Our wedding day.

But sometime between when I said the words to Nisha and now, a few blocks and a short walk, I knew how right my hand felt wrapped around hers, that whatever I felt for her was real. The freedom to choose who I wanted, rather than being persuaded by the sort of girl I was *supposed* to woo.

Nisha was different. And perfect.

Fuck me if I don't want her.

But with all my faults and the damage between us, would she still want me?

CHAPTER 6

NISHA

I CURLED IN THE RECLINER, draped in a soft squishy robe and sipped an iced tea–not the Long Island sort or I'd never be able to get up afterwards–while a lovely girl who's name I forgot curled my hair.

Forgot, because she was one of ten beauticians working on me like I was the bride, not a last minute date for the event. Mani, pedi, the whole basket of services and more primping and priming than I ever experienced in my life.

As Ford's date.

I swallowed too much iced tea and choked.

"Are you okay?" The slightly accented voice behind me asked, patting me in the wrong direction, encouraging the drink to go down when it was insistent on heading back up to find a convenient exit.

"Fine," I gasped at a rare pocket of air. My muscles worked, and I could breathe again.

"Alright, let's fix that." The hoard of helpers swarmed me, patting powder under my eyes where tears formed.

"Maybe we should have gone with waterproof mascara," I croaked, still trying to catch my breath.

"True."

The mascara was wiped off with oil soaked pads and fresh coats applied.

More powder. More priming.

"Better."

A mirror popped up in my field of vision.

"That's not me."

The team tittered at my not-joke while I tried to reconcile the honey goddess in the mirror with myself who yesterday dressed as Rudolph in green tights.

Finally my hair was curled and I walked up to the register, clutching the cuddly gown they insisted I keep, and clinging to the suit for Ford they delivered to me to take down for him.

"Now, don't let Mister Millham ruin your nice makeup when you deliver his suit," one of the girls finishing up tossed out to me.

My cheeks blazed under ten layers of foundation. "Oh, no. I'm just his date. We aren't– we're not–" I stumbled over my denial.

"Mhhm." The girl made an *as if* sound low in her throat. "Well, if you aren't now then you soon will be," she assured my shocked face, ushering me out the door and holding the lift for me.

I stepped inside the metal box, swiping the spare key Ford gave me and hit his floor. The elevator moved, along with my heart. Did I want to sleep with Ford? Because the way he looked at me, hell the way he *kissed* me, even though it was the briefest graze of cinnamon and sea salt, clenched my thighs together. Because the man did everything with intent.

Whether it was holding my hand, telling me his story, or

touching me…or buying dresses and pampering me like a princess.

I am just a date, I told myself firmly.

My pep talk didn't do shit.

Strangling the garment hanger, I counted doors on Ford's floor until I came to his and paused outside for a moment. There were no sounds from within, but then the doors were fairly thick. I raised my hand to knock before my frazzled brain remembered I had a key. Fumbling everything, I dropped the key, caught the garment bag mid air and managed not to end up tits over teakettle in the hallway.

Winning.

"Nisha?" Ford's voice rolled over my head.

"Here! Uh, it's me," I muttered, clutching the key hard enough to flex the card.

"You got my suit! You're such a freaking gem." He didn't sound half as delighted as his words made him seem.

"Uh, you're welcome? I didn't really organise much this time around."

The hanger disappeared from my hand and he propelled me inside. "Why are you wearing a towel?" he asked curiously.

I pulled my elf suit out of one of the oversized pockets along with my phone and set them on a stand. "It's the spa's. They put me in it, and you said I could dress in here?" *Right? He had said that, and I wasn't standing naked under a soft robe in his room for no reason?* I wanted to sink into the floor. "Are you sure this is a good idea, Ford?" I glanced down at his bed, then took in the view from his broad window. "Oh, my God. You can see everything from here."

"Everything I want." His voice lowered.

I spun on my heel to find him already in the shirt, though it hung open giving me the same tantalising view of Fordland with extra ink I glimpsed the day before. "You're not kidding," I said without thinking.

"True."

My gaze raised to his face. If I thought he wanted to devour me before, I was dead wrong. Because not only did he *look* edible, his eyes told me flat out how much he wanted what he saw right in front of him.

Then a shadow passed across his face, and the moment shattered.

"What happened?" I stepped into him, catching his cuffs and straightening them out. "Cufflinks. You have some, right?"

"Rex dropped them off an hour ago. I've got to go down for photos." He passed me a small box.

"Huh." I turned the sparkly studs in my hands and fixed them to his shirtsleeves. "I figure you can button yourself up."

"Nisha..." He caught my wrists in a firm grip and swallowed hard, his Adam's apple bobbing as he traced his gaze over my face and hair. "You're beautiful."

That damn blush shot up my neck and danced on my cheeks.

"It's a lot of makeup and colour and...things."

"I'd still like to see you with your hair down though. I want to brush it," he mused.

I swore my whole head *glowed.*

"Um, you said something about a dress," I whispered, studying the tops of his shiny dress shoes. When had those gone on? Did he strip behind me and I missed the whole thing because I was gawking at the *park?*

"Give me a sec." He disappeared into the walk in robe, and came out with a garment bag much like the one his suit came in, though this was white. "For you, ma'am."

"Don't you ma'am me," I threatened, smiling through my embarrassment. Ford's gaze weighed on me as I unzipped the top of the bag and peeked inside.

Miles of luxurious, shimmering forest green velvet

studded with what looked like diamonds filled the inside of the bag. I dipped a finger to touch the soft cowl neckline and sighed.

"You like it?" Ford stepped a little closer, wrapping my arms around the bag and pressing his fingertips between my shoulder blades. "Let me see it on you."

I swallowed hard. The dress must cost a fortune, and... "This is too much," I whispered. "I barely know you and I'll never repay you."

"I never asked to be repaid. In any way," Ford said firmly. "If you want to go home after tonight, to *your* home, without me...and never see me again, that's fine. I mean it's not, I'll be a lost, heartbroken wretch and all but you know," he affected a sniff, "it's fine."

"Dick," I muttered, elbowing his stomach.

"You'll crease the shirt," he warned me. "I have to be down there in less than half an hour. I don't want to rush you but you know...I really did buy that with you in mind, Nisha. I just hoped you'd say yes."

His words hung between us, their double meaning on a wedding day evident, even if the day belonged to someone else.

"I'll be right back." I retreated, bumping my back on the corner of the bathroom door and managing to make it inside and shut the door without suffering any further damage. Once I was inside, I dropped the robe from my shoulders and rubbed the sore spot. "Owww." I glanced over my shoulder ruefully. A small red mark bloomed beneath my skin. "Okay. I can do this."

"Does the dress talk back?" Ford called through the closed door.

"Let a girl dress," I admonished him lightly, stifling a laugh.

The man was *impossible*.

I hung the bag on the top of the dry shower glass, and

pulled the dress free. The floor length sheath was perfect. I slipped into it on my own, only needing a little help with the stubborn zipper, but Ford could assist with that in a moment. The cap shoulders sat slightly off centre, and the cowl hung between my breasts, dropping to a borderline low that exposed skin without the risk of a nip slip.

Diamontes sewn into the material glittered like fresh snow over the forest whenever I moved. *I'll have to dance in this.* A slit to mid thigh showed just enough skin to tease. It was probably time to tell Ford about my two left feet.

The dress made me feel beautiful, like he said I was, even if I was just still tour-guide Nisha in seasonal dress finding strays to help or bring home for Christmas dinner. After all, wasn't that what I did with Ford, to an extent? If the situation was somewhat reversed.

"Everything okay in there?" Ford knocked gently.

I pulled the door slightly ajar. "Can you help me with the zip, pretty please?" I begged, batting my eyelashes.

"How on earth am I going to refuse you anything?" he murmured, his voice low and deep.

Reindeer swooped in my stomach. "Guess I'll have to make outlandish demands on you then," I said dryly. "Starting with, could you please zip me up?" I quipped, turning my back to him.

Ford's hands grazed my shoulderblades, tracing along my spine to the base of the zip. Firm, sure hands closed around my waist as he did me up, standing close enough behind me that I could feel his heat against my back.

"I've gotta go downstairs. Do you–" He cleared his throat again, sliding one hand over my stomach and pulling me back into him. "Do you want to come with me, or stay up here? You don't have to come to a wedding for people you don't know."

"I know you," I managed, aching to lean back into his touch, and let him take all the fears that whirled around me, leaving me slightly lightheaded. Or maybe that was just his proximity.

"I got you a purse. I mean, the girl suggested it, and I agreed." He pushed a glittery beaded affair into my hands. "Your key for this room is in there already. You don't have to use it but…I want you to stay with me tonight."

I swallowed, letting my hand flutter over his on my stomach where the hooligan reindeer whooped and tore about in circles. "I'll see, okay?" I whispered, tilting my head back until I could see his face. "This is all new to me."

He smiled, a true, free smile I suspected was rare in his world, whatever world that was. Because sure as Santa hat wearing alpacas, Ford Millham was not the lost man I thought he was when I found him taming his spitty alpaca in the middle of NYC.

"I know. Come down with me?" He proffered his elbow.

Feeling like the world turned on without me, I took it, curving my fingers around the muscle beneath his suit jacket.

Maybe tonight could be something different. Like starlight and fairy godmother type dream stuff.

Maybe I'd stay with him after all.

CHAPTER 7

NISHA

THE WEDDING WAS AMAZING. Their families, and the couple.

After hanging out while team bride and groom did photos, I loved the atmosphere the affair created. And I couldn't keep my eyes off Ford Millham.

The moment he let go of my hand after finding me a seat in one of the back rows, his shoulders took on a hard line that hadn't been there before, his strides determined as he powered up the aisle.

But he slipped into the group of groomsmen chattering together easily enough, though I saw some differences between the man in his room versus the one I saw now. The muscle in his jaw flexed as he spoke to the groom, all of the wedding party looking so debonair.

I tugged my phone out of the beaded clutch he gave me, sending off a quick message to Denise, my fellow tour guide and neighbour to pick up the ham, the cherries and anything else we needed for Christmas breakfast tomorrow, and that I wouldn't be back til late if at all.

My phone blew up with her messages, and I rolled my eyes, ignoring most of them, especially when I admitted my door didn't lock anymore and was mostly stuck now. A good boot knocked it open and she could store everything in my fridge.

Then the music started and I welled up before anything happened. I sniffled, batting my eyelashes on the back of my hand so I didn't smear anything.

"This is why I hate weddings. I always cry." It was true. I'd been to three weddings in my life and ended up crying all over the mother of the bride in every single one of them. All school friends, and one ex-boyfriend who got married and invited me.

Yes, I still cried.

Emotions, huh?

"Here." An elderly lady slipped into the row beside me and offered me a monogrammed handkerchief.

"Oh. I can't, possibly–" I shook my head, pushing a hand away, but she insisted. Finally, I caved, smiling gratefully

"Are you friends with the groom?" my elderly neighbour asked.

I swiped at my eyelashes and below. Barely any colour came off onto the handkerchief in my hand. Thank God for waterproof mascara.

"No. I'm the date Ford…" I looked up, losing track of where they all stood and pointed him out. "He's my date. Just for tonight." Or I'm his. Was one more right than wrong? I puzzled over the phrasing for a moment.

"Oh, yes. They look so good." She folded her hands neatly on her lap, holding her bag there and faced forward.

"Are you family?" I asked, looking at the stylish little lady.

Her hair was shot with silver and twisted elegantly around her head, no dye jobs in sight. *Life goals.*

"Oh, no. I came in from the street." She nodded, smiling.

I paused. "You don't know them?" *No more than I do.*

"Oh, no. I like to go to weddings. It reminds me of my own wee man. He passed in the war." She grabbed her purse a little tighter

"Which war?" I asked without thinking. "I'm sorry."

"Don't apologize. To be honest, I don't even remember their names now. Just lots and lots of years gone by. Celebrate life. Celebrate love." She tapped me smartly on my knee.

I smiled. "I definitely need to do that."

"We all do." She grabbed my hand with her gnarled one, holding on tight.

Music swelled around us. We both turned to watch the bridesmaids' parade, but my attention kept drifting back to Ford, and I missed the bride completely.

His gaze flicked to me and held, and I was lost for a decent slice of time. When the bride and groom kissed, Ford had his groomsmen duties to attend to, and the contact broke, leaving me floundering. His attention found somewhere else and held.

A blonde in an ice blue dress and the boobs to fill it out waved at him from the opposite side of the aisle, grabbing my attention. He stared at her woodenly, his eyes hard, full of anger.

The emotions the wedding brought on were replaced by a tsunami of whatever Ford felt, hitting my chest hard. I gasped for breath, looking down to make a comment to my little old lady, but the spot beside me stood empty. I half rose, glancing over my shoulder at the door, but she disappeared as though she was never there at all.

I turned back in time to find Ford standing right in front of me. I let out a little croaking sound, and flew backwards.

"You're jumpy, Neesh," Ford murmured, sliding his arm across my lower back and crushing me against his chest. I grabbed his shirt, remembering too late that I wasn't supposed to crinkle it and let go. "It's okay. I could use a hug." He rolled his shoulders, the muscle still ticking in his jaw.

"Is that where this relationship is going? You pay me, and I provide you a service? That's not very romantic," I admonished him.

The biddies in the row behind gasped.

I really didn't care, especially as Ford's grim face split in a broad grin.

"Can you be sassier?"

"You have no idea." I toyed with the buttons on the shirt, looking up at him. "So, what happens now? Have you got groomsmen duties to go to?"

"I do. We've already done photos, but I think there's more on some other stuff –" He waved a hand vaguely backward toward where the rest of the party called out to him. "I'll be a second," he yelled out over the crowd.

With a start, I was forcibly reminded of him yelling word out 'cock' in the middle of the Plaza foyer.

He turned back to me, catching my wrist and tracing over my fluttering pulse. "Tell me you'll come back to my room with me tonight."

The biddies gasped again.

"I– I want to," I whispered, making the decision before I was ready.

"You're so fucking cute," Ford growled.

A muted thump hit the floor behind us.

I giggled. "Go, before you have a heart attack."

"Tonight," Ford murmured, ignoring my warning completely. "I want quiet hours. Just you and me." He dipped his head and when I thought he might kiss me, he dropped his forehead to gently rest against mine. "I've got stuff to do.

There's a bar," he pointed out, then which door the reception would be held at with a list of times.

"It's okay. I'll find you, or something." I wiggled the key card from my purse.

Another muffled thump and I swore someone fainted.

Ford sorted. "See you later. Don't forget."

Hesitating for a second, he brushed his lips gently across mine, and then he was gone, my legs buckling, and I was glad I didn't hit the floor like the lady behind me.

"Sorry about that." I called over my shoulder. Tracing my fingertip over my mouth where he kissed me, I decided it was time to find the bar.

.

APART FROM SEEING Ford dance with his bridesmaid, I barely caught more than a glimpse of him for the entire reception. A group of girls pulled me in to dance the macarena as I loitered by the cake stand for the umpteenth time, and I thankfully missed the bouquet when I got myself herded into that group too. The flowers hurtled, I ducked, and someone else was the lucky recipient.

More than once I fingered the card in my beaded purse–Ford's, really, because I didn't pay for a thing. By the time the dance floor filled with drunken party-goers and bridesmaids flirting up a storm with their dates while the groomsmen chartered away boisterously–sans Ford– I was ready to take my elf-ass upstairs, slip back into the clothes I left bundled beside the bed, and head home.

Until Ford burst out of a doorway at the rear of the room, stalking across the back of the dance floor. His hair was a mess, his shirt half undone. He hit the bar, leaning over it to grab a bottle of whiskey. When the barman objected, he threw a wad of cash at him. The barman's face widened in shock as he flicked through the bills.

I know how you feel.

I sympathise with the poor man; Ford on a rampage was a formidable force. But the man was hurting and considering how much time he took on me, I wanted to be able to repay something in kind. Also, I couldn't leave the man aching.

I detached myself from my space of wall, heading in his direction, but a scarlet tipped hand halted my progress.

"Oh, I wouldn't bother him when he's in a mood like this, sweetie," a sugary voice laid the condensation on thick.

I pivoted to find a blonde with a fixed smile and eyebrows stuck with so much botox they didn't move staring determinedly at me in the ice blue dress I noticed waving at him at the wedding.

"I don't think–"

"You're after Ford. He does this kind of thing often. Well, me." She gave a tinkle of a laugh that could have scratched glass with its diamond hard edges. "So leave him alone, I mean, to me, will you? Whatever fling," she scraped her gaze over me, "you had going on is done now. Run along." She made a dismissive gesture with her fingers, flicking them so close to my face I wanted to bite off one of her fake nails.

I shook my head as a mountain of a man with bulging muscles that seemed to move on their own approached her with two glasses of champagne. To my surprise, he offered one to me.

"Thank you," I murmured, my brow creasing, wondering if I shouldn't drink it.

"Don't give it to her!" the blonde half-shrieked.

The image of an untidy, seething Ford ripping his way through the room met the facade of the ice queen at my side.

"You're the jilter," I said quietly without thinking.

A comment that should never have been heard, but it fell

in one of those lulls of conversation that everyone in the vicinity was privy to.

"What?" The girl stared at me, clutching the stems of both champagne glasses so hard I thought they'd snap.

I don't have time for you.

"Excuse me," I murmured, flashing a sympathetic smile at the large man who offered me a drink.

He seemed surprised to be addressed at all and shot me a blindingly white, winning smile. "Merry Christmas," he offered.

I murmured something similar, turning my back on the odd couple in a bid to locate Ford before I lost him again for the night, but a sharp gasp pulled me back.

"Did *he* do this?" the girl cried dramatically. "He threatened me in the lift, too, you know."

I blinked, making the mistake of turning back. "Ford hasn't touched me."

Her cruel smile struck me at heart level. "Oh, that's right. The dates were a bet."

"What?" I swallowed, backing up a step. "I have to go."

"You're right, Cinderella, it's midnight and the ball is over. So is your time with him." She raised an eyebrow. "Poor local girl thought she could play with the big man."

I closed my eyes. "You know, I always hated uppity bitches like you at school." Breathing out, I heard her huff and by the time I opened my eyes, I stood alone, though several of the other wedding guests stared openly.

After the little scene the girl I suspected was Ford's ex just created, I didn't blame them.

My dress was too exposing and too tight all at once. I pushed through the crowd that seemed never ending, seeking Ford, a door, an exit...*anything.* I found a gap and shot through it, managing to slip around a waiter carrying a tray of champagne flutes and dodging a woman supporting a drunk man–one of the groomsmen, maybe?--I didn't pause to look. The door was there, and I disappeared into the open air, gasping like a fish out of water.

Four people huddled in a small group chattering watched me like I was a time bomb about to explode.

"Are you okay?" one of the men asked, stepping forward.

I spied the lift with its open doors, and raised a hand. "No, thank you. Hold the lift!" I called, taking off on the sky high heels my feet were so not used to wearing.

The figure turned in the lift as I skittered inside, and I found myself the sole recipient of a hard, blue gaze no longer twinkling like morning sunlight on fresh snow.

Ford.

"I see you've met Jess," he said, swiping a hand through his already unruly hair. His lips formed a tight line, but my gaze drifted to his rumpled shirt and open bow tie.

"Did you get claustrophobic?" I asked softly.

"When she launched herself at me?" He barked a harsh laugh. "Yeah, you could say I got upset. Couldn't get her claws out of me. As per fucking usual."

I nodded, playing with the beads on my purse. "I'm out of my league with this high society stuff, Ford. I'm just a girl in an elf suit who loves Chrismtas and the city she lives in. I don't do…catfights, or whatever the hell this is devolving into." My voice stayed quiet and clear, and I was damn proud of myself.

"It is highschool level bullshit," he agreed, and sighed, holding out a hand. "Tell me I can still convince you to stay with me." His voice turned husky. "Tonight isn't a night I want to be alone. Her touch…" He shuddered.

That's a terrible reason to stay.

Heedless of my brain, I placed my hand in his and the moment his fingers curled around mine, he tugged me a little closer, his eyes darkening.

"Stay, Nisha," he whispered.

A shiver rippled over my skin and I wrapped my arms around myself. "This is a really bad idea."

"You don't want me?" He tilted his head to one side.

"You have way too much confidence, Mister Millham," I said tartly, pulling my hand free and tapping his chest. A very hard, muscular, and swoon worthy chest.

Get your act together, Miss Lister.

"It comes with the territory." He stepped closer and I shifted back, a dance we continued until my back hit the flat mirror finish at the side of the elevator car.

"I don't fit into your territory, Ford." I lifted my gaze to him, begging him to step back though I couldn't make myself say it. I wanted the same thing as he did far too much.

The elevator door dinged open, a soft announcement that meant I had a decision to make.

CHAPTER 8

FORD

Nisha's dark eyes were like pools of starlight as she stared up at me, swathed in the green dress that was hers the moment I set eyes on it the afternoon before. Hell, she should have knocked me back when I asked her to be my date for the wedding, and here I was pushing her for more.

I was lucky she didn't slap me.

Or maybe she should have. In the end, it didn't matter, because before she could say a word, I cupped her chin between my fingers and kissed her.

Nisha froze on the spot. Half a second, maybe less. That was all it took for my life to go to hell. Not a single breath passed, then her mouth softened against mine, and she welcomed the kiss.

I scooped her against me, walking us backwards to my room, breaking away only to make sure I had the right one before I swiped my keycard from my pocket and pushed the door open.

Nisha mewled softly at the lack of contact. I grinned at her, keeping a firm hold. There was no way she was getting away from me at this point. Unless she said no, but the way her lips parted, those big eyes even larger, sucking in my soul…

"Greedy girl," I murmured, swooping down for another kiss.

"Pushy man," she laughed, pushing me back. Her chin tipped up, and the few free strands of her curled hair hung along the curve of her shoulders.

"Am I?"

"Mmhmm. Do I have to make a list?"

"Only if I'm on the naughty side."

She groaned. "Stop, please. That was terrible."

"It was," I agreed, spinning her on the spot. "I've been dying to see your hair out. May I?" I brushed my fingertips over the pins that held her chignon up.

She nodded jerkily, grasping the beaded clutch in front of her. I leaned over her, tugging the bag free and tossed it onto a gold velvet chintz chair. My other hand worked at the pins, tugging them free gently so I didn't pull any of the long strands. Finally I unrolled the black mass, running my fingers through the silky strands, and let her hair tumble down her back.

"So beautiful," I murmured.

She cast a glance over her shoulder. "I'm nervous as hell, Ford."

Alarm bells rang for me. I curved my palm around her cheek, fitting her back to my chest and held her there. "Tell me you've done this before and I'm not pushing you in ways I shouldn't," I demanded, searching her stunning face.

She shook her head, and raised her eyes to meet mine. "It's not my first time, Ford. But this isn't something I do. You know. Hotel rooms. A wealthy man." Her brow pinched and I held my breath waiting for the question she would inevitably ask, but the question never eventuated. "Falling in lust."

"Is that that this is?" My heart ached at the sentiment–or lack thereof–in her speech. "Just lust?"

She laughed softly, turning to face me, linking her hands behind my neck. "What else can it be, Ford? I live here. You're going home, halfway around the world in a few days. Lust… it's enough?" The question tripped off her tongue and she closed her eyes on a sigh. "I'm sorry."

I caught her chin, lifting her face back to mine. "Don't be." I kissed her again. "At all." More kisses. "I feel the same damn way." I kissed her a little hard this time, hooking my fingers under the sleeves of the velvet gown she wore and tugging gently. "If you aren't ready for this I'd love to just hold you and fall asleep."

A total lie, but I wasn't aiming to be the asshole with every girl I met. Maybe just Jess. I pushed my conniving ex from my mind, focusing on the girl before me. Woman. Because… curves. And honey skin. And those kissable damn lips. I groaned. Gathering her into my arms, I kissed us both stupid.

When I came to my senses, we were half sprawled across the enormous bed, making out like a pair of teens.

"Come on, honey." I slid my hands beneath Nisha's body, grazing the curve of her hip and squeezing. "Let's do this right."

I drew back enough to look into her face. No way did I want to hurt this girl who'd held my shit together for me when she could barely hold herself together.

Sure, on the outside she looked all organised, seeing people she knew, taking her tours with the ferry timetables lodged in her head. But beneath that was a skittish girl who turned at every new shiny thing that dashed past…like a lost Aussie and his alpaca in the middle of the city.

A girl I was fast falling for.

"Help," she murmured, wiggling hr hips and, it seemed, doing her damdest to torture me. "I'm stuck."

"I can tell." My voice came out rough, and her eyes shot to my face. "Sorry, just…you wiggle real well, beautiful."

"I–oh." Her lips rolled together and she looked down where she shimmied against my too-tight jeans. NIsha licked her lips. "You mean like this?" She wiggled again, and damn if I didn't roll us both so she was on top.

My hands slid beneath her dress, teasing the curve of her ass with my fingertips. "Yeah, just like that." I sucked in a long breath and held it, desperate to regain some sense of sanity. "Let me take this dress off you." I flexed my hands, desperate to rip the material from her and sink balls deep, but I didn't think she'd appreciate that side of me either.

Or maybe I was wrong, and she would.

Nisha shook her head, her black hair slinking around her shoulders with a life of its own. "No. You get to watch."

She bit her lip as she reached around, snagging the zip. My mouth was half open to object that she couldn't reach on her own, when the sound of its rasp filled the room.

The little minx could do that thing on her own.

A goofy-ass smile spread across my lips as I watched her shimmy out of her sleeves and begin to lower the dress like she was unwrapping the best Christmas present I'd ever gotten.

The tops of her breasts came into view, honeyed domes that left me drooling on the bed a little. I swiped the back of my hand across my mouth when she paused, looking up at me through her lashes. *Out of practice my ass.*

"Keep going," I begged softly, adjusting my cock through my jeans.

Her smile bordered on pure sin as the dress fell to the floor and she stretched with her hands overhead like a kitty just waking up.

"Better?" she asked, her hips swaying in a mesmerising rhythm.

I crooked my finger at her, leaning back on the bed. "Closer."

Her gaze fixed on me as the words I said to her today—yesterday, hells I didn't know what day it was, I was so lost in her—she stepped forward, swinging her hips, the tips of her hair brushing the top of her gorgeous ass.

When she reached me, wearing only a thong and her heels, she swung a knee up either side of my waist and sank down on me.

Even with my suit pants and her lacy thong between us, I could feel her heat. My hands closed on her hips and I jerked her into me, crushing her lips with my for an instant before I softened the kiss. "I want to spank you, be rough as hell with you because for the last two days the idea of you being right here," I pulled her closer, grinding our bodies together as her hair draped around us like a black curtain to a private show, "has consumed me."

"Mmmm, so you only wanted my body."

I shrugged. "I'd say no but...I want you. So fucking badly." I kissed her again, sweeping my tongue across her lips, waiting for her response. Nisha gasped, her lips parting, and I took that as permission, kissing her thoroughly until she moaned into my mouth. "Perfect."

"Mmhmm." She made a little whimper, rolling her hips over mine. "Are we getting to the 'clothes off' stage now?" she whispered against my lips.

"Smart ass." I slapped her rump for the hell of it, enjoying the tiny sound she made in protest far too much.

"May I?" She stared at me as she slithered off my lap, tumbling between my legs.

I reached out to catch her, exhaustion and alcohol stopping me from actually catching her. "Are you okay?"

"Yep." Her hands slid along the insides of my thighs, and she nuzzled her perfect lips against my groyne. "Please?"

"Whatever you want," I gasped as she lowered my zipper with her teeth. Her tongue enveloped me as the fact I preferred to freeball became abundantly clear. Right before she–

Her warm, liquid hot mouth covered my length, and my head fell back onto the bed. One hand tangled in her hair as she worked me, and I tried hard not to thrust up into her mouth, only failing to hold onto my resolve a few times. When the familiar tingle at the base of my spine grew too much, I pulled her up my body, breathing hard.

"Girl, I'm feeling overdressed."

Nisha smiled, licking her lips and started to unbutton my shirt while I worked at cufflinks I swore weren't doing their job, or maybe they did the job too well. In the end I tore one off, the diamond studded metal pinging across the room. The other came free and I shucked my shirt off, catching her thighs and drawing her up my body until I could lick the tender flesh inside her legs.

"Wait–"Nisha gave a startled cry, tumbling forward but I caught her.

"Hold yourself up," I admonished. "For as long as you can."

I prayed I was up to the task. Nisha wasn't the only one it might have been awhile for. After last Christmas, I hadn't wanted anyone else at all...until Nisha torpedoed into my life, catching us up in a tangle of santa hats and Christmas lights.

And no part of having my own personal Christmas treat wrapped around me made me want to let her go. *Ever.*

Fuck me, I'm falling for a girl I can't have.

The realisation slammed into me as I flicked my tongue out to taste her slicked need that coated my lips. Her cry mingled with my goran as I ate her slowly, savouring though my desire for her bordered on ravenous. Insatiable.

Stull, I held back, managing to rein in my own need until her hips rocked over my face and she came with the most delicious cry I etched into my memories to keep forever.

Her thighs trembled as I tipped her gently sideways, kicking off my pants and shoes, and reaching for my wallet.

I pulled out a condom, tearing the corner slightly as she held out her hands. "May I?"

Bemused, I nodded as she pulled herself up on shaking arms, her trembling hand encircling my cock. "Tell me I haven't worn you out already, beautiful," I murmured against her neck, licking at the salty drops there, nipping the hollow of her shoulder.

She shrieked, wriggling against me as she worked the rubber on over my cock. I dropped a hand between her legs, two fingers gliding effortlessly inside, teasing until her hands dropped away from me and she fell back amidst the fluffy white bedding.

I arched over her, notching myself at her entrance and pushed in a little. Her eyes flared wide as I pushed my hips forward, kissing her to forestall.

"Unless you're telling me no right now, Nisha, I promise I'lll go slow. After that though…" I breathed hard through my nose, holding her gaze.

"Don't hurt me?" she whispered.

I cradled her face in my hands. "Promise, honey. I won't hurt you." *Not like this.*

Resting my forehead against hers, I inched my way inside her heat, groaning as her pretty little pussy pulsed around my invading cock. Her soft whimpers drove me until I seated myself fully inside her.

"You feel so good," she whispered, her voice straining already.

"I want to make you scream," I ground out, gripping her hip tight. With effort, I gave her a few gentle thrusts, noting what made her cry out softly, what made her shudder. Her arms wrapped around my neck, and she nibbled my ear as I caught one knee, tugging her body lower, spearing into her deeper.

"Stop holding back on me, Ford," she whispered, her tongue curled around my ear lobe.

I let out a low moan, snapping my hips deeper. She arched until our hips ground together. My thrusts became harder, faster as I worked our bodies together. Everything felt perfect; the way she fit against me, her soft, ragged breaths kissing my lips. The taste of her sweat and her desire on my tongue.

Nisha clenched tight around me, her long, drawn out moan the perfect accompaniment to the sounds I couldn't hold back either. She came on a cry, her body softening as she sank into my embrace, her mouth grazing mine as she left out the sweetest little sound I ever heard.

That was the point my control snapped.

I pounded into her soft body, gripping the iron railing behind the bed, my other hand closed around her hip for purchase as I drove myself and her closer to the next orgasmic wave. She shuddered beneath me as my balls drew up tight.

I could love this girl every goddamn night for the rest of my life.

My orgasm slammed into me, almost painful with its intensity. I roared my need to the darkness before I crashed into Nisha, my arms wrapped around her, cradling her close as she weathered her own pleasure, along with my torment.

Then we fell together.

CHAPTER 9

NISHA

Strong hands worked their way along my thighs, spreading me open. I woke to Ford's lips pressed to my aching flesh that should be too tender from his brand of sweet and rough love the night before. My eyes fluttered open as his tongue traced its way along the insides of my thighs and filled me with hot, wet flesh. Drawn from a dream of his hands on me, all over me, my body pulsed hard as sleep was ripped from me, replaced with the erotic feeling of a mouth on my pussy as I woke.

I whimpered, one hand covering my mouth, the other gripping the sheets in my fist.

"Already?" Ford's tongue withdrew, and he lapped at my swollen skin. "Christ, you taste like Chriastmass morning," he whispered reverently, soothing my lady bits as I shuddered in his hands. "Let's see if we can do that again."

"Huh?" I lifted my drowsy head from the pillows, staring down at him where his head popped up comically from between my legs. Morning light slanted through the large windows, leaving us in the pale facade of a glow under the suite's heating. I shivered, clutching at the sheet and pulling it up but Frod frowned, grabbing the other side in a game of tug-o-war I was never going to win.

"No. You're beautiful, and I want to see you." *While I still can.*

The unspoken time limit between us encroached by the second, and I caved. Or maybe it was the way his other hand stroked the insides of my thighs, tracing the patterns his tongue left there a minute before.

"Okay," I whispered, releasing my grip on the sheets and finding his hand instead.

Ford's grip was firm and reassuring as he wormed his way back to his place, lapping and licking me until I left crescent moon shapes on the back of his hand.

"Sorry," I gasped, curling in on myself. "I mean–"

I half expected him to pull me back, expose me to his intense gaze again while snow drifted across the window outside. The luxury of being so warm and naked in the glistening reflected light on Christmas Eve morning left me lightheaded.

But Ford did none of what I expected, holding true to form. Instead, his magnificent, ripped body rose over me. He braced one taut forearm over my head, leaning down to kiss me deeply as I tasted myself on his lips. The erotic, slippery feel left me writhing a little beneath him, though his body barely contacted mine.

I did use the opportunity to perv on my unexpected lover, running my hands along his biceps to his shoulders, memorising the hard lines and deep curves of his musculature.

"No wonder you looked so good in that suit last night," I

muttered, tracing over his pecs and tapping Pickles' face. "Won't he be jealous?"

Ford stared down at me. "Is that what you think?"

I didn't get to answer before he kissed me again, a little harder than before, and I couldn't work out which question he answered, or if he answered anything at all.

This man is a master at evasion.

And a few other things.

When he drew back I was breathless, and my hands continued their Mister Millham tour all on their lonesome. I stopped over the fingers of ink I'd seen tantalising flashes of before, and traced over them but they weren't the tribal ink I thought. More like a road map….or something digital.

Deus nolans exituus.

I frowned, reading the words inked into his flesh. "God… doesn't want. No. That's wrong. My Latin is crap. Uh, something about forever results?"

"Get results, whether God is willing or not," Ford translated softly. "I decided at twenty I no longer wanted to put my fate in others' hands, and wanted to take control."

My heart wept for him. "What–" His face closed and I changed tack. "Why the computer parts?" I tilted my head to one side. "Not computer…more like a robot."

He grinned. "I couldn't decide between that and *deus ex machina*, god from the machine. So I took a bit of both."

"Of course you did," I said dryly as he laughed above me. "Mister Skynet."

But the dual meaning, taking hold of his own destiny without anyone else's help required, being the unexpected voice within the machine that conquered all…it suited him.

And I felt very small and frivolous beneath him.

"Am I that terrifying?" he asked softly, dipping his head to kiss along my throat, over my collarbone.

I wiggled at the tickling sensation. "No. Just…I feel small, next to you. You've got everything going on. I'm just a girl who tries to bring a little Christmas spirit in a city that sometimes forgets the meaning."

"And you don't see that as a critical function?" His brow creased. "Because I see magic in what you do, and who you are. It's one of the reasons I'm–" He froze above me, his face a mask.

I shifted. "Yeah. Terrifying. Utterly."

He laughed again, trailing one hand along my side and gripped my hip, flipping me over. I squealed as I face planted in the soft bedding, the warmth of it sucked from my body and then wrapped around me in a dizzying inverted motion. Cold air assailed my back for a moment before Ford's weight settled over me.

"Oh–" I shuddered at the contact.

One arm slid between me and the bedding as he gathered me close, his nose brushing along my throat, his tongue flicking the shell of my ear. "So fucking beautiful. So full of energy and magic and chaos. You're everything I want."

Breath left me at the declaration. "You're going to give me a god complex," I whispered into the sheets. "Or at least an elf one." I turned my head, resting my cheek on the pillow ford pulled beneath me, and clung to his arm.

Foil crackled and his knee slid between my thighs, pushing my legs apart.

"Wrap your hands around my arm, Nisha." His voice was low and rough, caressing the back of my neck in an undeniably intimate gesture. Hairs rose three and I shivered.

"Why?"

"Because you're going to need to hold on."

"I am?" The head of his cock nudged my entrance, and I gasped.

"Yeah." His voice turned low and gravelly as he gripped my hip, lifting me and slammed home.

Ford told the truth: I needed to hold on.

I clutched his arm like a lifeline as he railed me, pausing to lick sweat from my shoulders or bite the tender spot at the join of my neck gently. Every breath that left me came out as a mewl, our melded noises animalistic and wild and wanton.

My body tightened as his thrusts grew rougher, his weight pressing me into the bedding.

"Come for me, Nisha. I want to feel your pretty little pussy flutter around my cock."

I whimpered, his dirty talk ripping pleasure through me. Releasing my cry into the pillow, I arched, chasing the roiling sensations as he pummelled his hips into me, burying himself deep and came with his own roar against my skin.

"So beautiful." Ford sank over me, his breath coming hard against my back. "Am I hurting you?" He reached between us, removing the condom and tying it off with a talented hand.

"Nope. Don't move, 'kay?" I murmured, tucking his arm beneath my cheek and breathing in the scent of us together.

"Christmas morning, Nisha. I'll never forget the taste of you."

My heart exploded and crashed all at once.

———

SOME TIME later when Ford's breaths evened and deepened, my brain decided it was time to leave. I pulled the sheet back one-handed, wiggling slowly to extract myself from God's embrace. Not an easy thing, when I didn't actually want to go. I didn't care right then that we had a limited amount of time between us\. I wanted to stay curled up in his arms and pretend everything was perfect.

"Don't leave, beautiful," he murmured, turning over and taking me along with him. His long, calloused fingers wrapped around my ankle, tugging me back to the embrace I welcomed far too readily.

Despite him foiling my plan to do exactly what he predicted, I giggled, shying away the logical part of my brain that muttered curses at my heart. "You are impossible."

"And you're sexy as all hell, Neesh. Come back. I want to sleep with you."

"You just did," I said softly, picking at his fingers that refused to release my ankle, wiggling my shoulders in the hold of his other arm.

"Nu-uh." He pulled sharply, drawing me across the bed.

I was still laughing and not really fighting when both inked arms wrapped around me, trapping my back to his chest, the now-familiar thump of his heart beating in time with mine, a rhythm to which I dozed.

"You're not running away from me tomorrow either, okay, elf girl? I've got plans."

"They better not include a flight to Australia." I yawned. "Because a hot Christmas and I do not go together."

"Nope. Something better." The pure joy in his voice rocked me.

"What?" *Am I getting a matching Pickles tattoo?*

The smile in his voice was evident, he trailed his hands along my back, tucking me into his side like a missing piece of the jigsaw puzzle that was him.

"You'll see."

THE TABLES TURNED as Ford dragged me across the road out the front of the Plaza on Christmas Eve. He plied me with hot chocolate and warm cookies, proclaiming it the most effective breakfast for a day out while I looked on suspiciously, but still chewed my cookie. I mean, warm Snickerdoodles were too good to give up.

"What have you got planned?" My suspicions grew as he stopped out the front of the Rockefeller Centre. The line that should be around the block was conspicuously absent. "What have you done, Ford?" I planted a hand on my hip, popping it out cause I knew he loved my sass, even if he cussed me for it.

Not that I wasn't dressed for the occasion, wearing the thick tights, boots, long sleeved top with jacket and matching mittens he had delivered with our breakfast, shooing me into the bathroom to change while he took time to check on Pickles. Weirdly, I missed the large alpaca that until yesterday seemed to be glued to Ford's side.

"Just wanted to say thank you for putting up with me for the last few days. I'm a bit of a diva and all, you know," he said absently, towing me inside and speaking quietly to the attendant who blinked at him and closed the door behind us.

I stared at the empty rink, completely devoid of people on the busiest day of their year, my voice on repeat. "What did you *do?*" I asked in a hushed voice.

"You don't need to whisper," he murmured, tucking my hair behind my ear. "There's no one here to hear us."

"I think that's kind of the point," I hissed, unable to drop my awe at seeing the giant space, usually so populated. "You must have…how much did this cost you?" I stared up at him, releasing all those questions I pushed away that should have been asked before I crawled into bed with an incredibly attractive and powerful man I didn't know.

"Does it matter?" He shrugged as though booking the Rockefeller ice rink at Christmas was nothing at all. Kind of like booking out Disneyland, a stunt usually reserved for royals…or the revoltingly rich.

I got the impression Ford wasn't the former, though I could be wrong.

"It does," I said warily as an attendant walked toward me with a pair of customised, brand new ice skates.

Ford slid me a sideways glance. "I cheated. I used your shoe size to guess."

"You did, huh?" It hit me how much effort he put into the morning's date, rather than just money that clearly didn't mean the same to him as it did to mean. Time, that is.

"Yeah." He wrapped an arm around me and nuzzled my hair sheepishly. Or alpacas? "I wanted to have you to myself. Last night...hell, Nisha. I'd repeat that every night if I got the chance."

"Oh," I sighed, letting Ford sweep me away in his fantasy land where there were only the two of us, a few staff, and a giant Christmas tree glowing merrily away.

He shooed the attendant away and took the boots, sliding them on my feet and doing the laces up with deft fingers. Naturally, they fit perfectly, just like everything else about him.

"Are you an unlikely alpaca sheikh? I think it's time you came clean about a few things," I said quietly, unwilling to pop my bubble, but also needing a few answers.

"Just enjoy it. And alpaca sheikh sounds good. I should put that on my business card. Right next to 'alpaca stud'." He grinned and pulled me to my feet. "How well can you skate?"

I stood slightly unsteadily. "It's been over a year. I wouldn't say my skills are phenomenal." But I also wouldn't be sliding across the ice on my butt any time soon. "Don't expect me to do pirouettes," I warned him.

"Dang it and I thought we'd be doing jumps by the end of the day."

My jaw dropped. "You booked the Rockefeller out for a day?" My voice rose to screech owl level.

Laughing, Ford wrapped an arm around my waist, pulling

my wobbling feet into him, along with the rest of me. "How are you feeling?"

I peered up at him. "Is this a trick question?"

His eyes danced, but the line of his mouth softened. "I know I'm a bit much. But I've learned to go for what I want, because these moments, like this one, they're fleeting." Ford skated backward for a bit until I found my balance. "Good to see it comes back to you."

"I thought you didn't live in the States," I scoffed. "And I thought you lived in a desert. How many ice rinks do they have in Australia?"

"Never seen one," he answered me cheerfully, pulling me into a slow circle that grew ever tighter. His hands dropped to my waist, his gaze on my tingling lips.

While my mind was stuck on how heart broken the man before me who could move literal Christmas Tree covered mountains was, he kissed me. After last night and again this morning, I should have been used to the feel of his mouth on mine. But Ford Millhams kisses covered a wide spread of ground and my feet weren't anywhere near it when I was in his arms.

His lips grazed mine, his mouth settling gently over my skin in the kind of kisses that left me floating. I slid my hands under his jacket, wrapping around the back of his neck and pulled him closer, but Ford didn't give into my growing need.

For a man who created epic impromptu dates and growled his own need over me all night long, he sure as hell had a great handle on his control right when I wanted it to fray.

His soft laugh against my mouth set my body alight with snowflake kisses. "Eager, little elf girl?"

"Maybe you didn't do quite the job you thought you did earlier," I teased him right back, smiling stupidly because–Ford. There was no other reason right now.

"Is that so?" He skated us in a slow, long arc as his eyes darkened. "Maybe I'll have to fix that later."

His promise settled between us as he led me close, his arms wound around my body. Like last night, we fit together perfectly, even with the added height of the ice skates. I rested my head against his shoulder as he led us around the ice, skating backward the entire time with no fear of anyone crashing into us. Music played softly around us, winding the perfect CHristmas ambiance over the ice.

I tilted my head back to stare up at the tree as we passed. "It's beautiful. I'm usually so engrossed with counting my tour numbers and making sure everyone is having a good time that I forget..." I bit my lip, letting my unfinished thought trail off.

I am a sad, sad person.

"Because you never take time to worry about yourself," Ford said. His fingers played in my long hair that trailed along my back, tugging the strands that shifted beneath my beanie until I looked up at him. "When was the last time you did something for yourself? Something I didn't organise...or anyone else." He stared at me and I realised we never did have that *are you single* conversation. The same thought must have occurred to him.

"We're a mess," I murmured.

"Yup, you're contagious." Ford smirked, though a shadow flickered behind his eyes.

"There isn't anyone else to make me take time for me, Ford," I whispered. "I haven't been on a date in years, let alone had anyone do something like what you did for me yesterday...today."

"It's just money." He shrugged, staring at some unknown point over my head.

How hurt has he been?

After meeting Jess, I had a bit of an idea what sort of woman he dated before, and how hard it bit his ass.

"No, it's more than that and don't you dare play it down," I said fiercely. "This took effort and more than a little persuading, Ford. Hell, even if it was just your dream thing to do with someone then I'm glad we're sharing it."

He looked down at me, his lips softening. The shadow behind his eyes lightened, their twinkle returning. "I wasn't doing it for only me." He threw his head back and laughed while I revseed us in a gentle circle and took the lead, my feet finally remembering how to skate. "That sounds utterly selfish. I once thought I'd love to do this. The whole New York, white Christmas affair thing with a girl I love in my arms." He dropped that bombshell with an easy grin that rounded up the reindeer inhabiting my insides nicely. "I met you three days ago, and I can't imagine doing this with anyone else. Not ever, Nisha. Your smile lights me up from the inside out. You make me remember what it feels like to play. Let go."

I started humming. "Should I call you Elsa? I'll get you a pretty costume," I offered with a sly smile. "Truely, I'm grateful to share this with you. You– everything. I live here, have only ever lived in New York City, and this is magic I haven't felt since I was a kid wondering when Santa would come."

"That's a fantasy we can play later, if it's what you want," Ford said thoughtfully, spinning us around until I didn't know who was leading any more.

"You have a filthy mind, Mister Millham," I said as he found my hand and spun me about slow enough I didn't lose my bearings.

Every second drew out until time froze as the tiniest snowflakes fell, scattering across our clasped hands, leaving us in the perfect snowglobe moment. Ford wrapped his hand around the back of my neck, drawing me in for a kiss that lasted forever and was still not anywhere near enough.

When I drew back, a teensy snowflake sat on the end of his

nose. Risking my balance I held onto his shoulders for purchase and licked the tip of his nose.

Ford blinked.

"That was unexpected."

We looked at each other as the snow began to dissipate, then as one, tipped our heads back and stuck out our tongues.

"Ahhh."

CHAPTER 10

FORD

THE MOMENT we left the Rockefeller Centre with our skates tied together over my shoulder, Nisha turned in the direction of the plaza hotel. I watched her wander off a few steps before our connected hands pulled tight.

"Huh?" She looked up at me all dreamily.

My heart plummeted, heading straight for her feet and prayed I wasn't falling alone.

"Did you think that was it?" I asked, only a little mocking, though that was mainly aimed at myself.

"A cleared out date skating beneath the tree isn't enough?" She looked at me with wide eyes. "I think there's such a thing as too much, Ford."

Her voice dropped to a whisper I barely heard as I reeled her back to me. Like hell was I letting go of the girl who matched my whirlwind fervour.

"There's really not."

I tugged her to my chest, dipping my head and kissed her

slowly as the Center's doors opened for the public, who merged around us curiously. A flash went off somewhere, but I ignored it.

"Make your own fate, huh?" she muttered into my jacket, burying her face there for a second, breathing deeply.

"Did I break you?" I stole the moment, tucking it away in my memories. Her beanie sat askew, and I buried my hand in her silky hair, cupping the back of her head and holding her there.

One perfect day.

It was all I wanted. But now I had that with her...I also knew I wanted more. So much more, and neither of us could easily give that.

But did it matter if something didn't come easily for once? That I might have to work my ass off for the girl I was fast falling for?

Three days doesn't not make a lifetime of heartstring.s

No, I knew all too well how that one went. A year later, the ghost of my last relationship screw-up still haunted me.

"Okay, so what have you got on your mind, Aussie?" Nisha grinned up at me, her cheekiness resumed.

The memory of her writhing beneath me hours before, the taste of her sweat on my tongue replaced the little smart ass, and I kissed her again, harder than before. When I drew back, she stared up at me, barely breathing. Her gloved hand rose to touch her mouth but I caught her wrist, pulling her impossibly close.

"No. Don't wipe that away. I want you to remember my kisses," I said a bit rough. Too rough, as her eyes widened and my cock fought a brief, relentless battle with my zipper. "I want you to remember," I murmured, squeezing her waist.

She nodded, leaning into me as I slung an arm around her and turned us in the direction of the park.

"Tell me something about you from home, Ford." She laced

her gloved fingers stiffly through mine at her shoulder as we walked. "Something that's not alpaca related. Something about just you."

"Something just me." I thought for a bit. "I grew up in the city on the other side of the county. In Sydney. Everything was always a little too close, and a little too busy."

"Gee, you must love it here." she said, dryly.

I poked her shoulder. "Let me finish, you impatient elf."

"Fine," she grumbled cutely, nestling into my side.

"So when I got the chance to visit an uncle in Western Australia, I took it. Learned how hot as Hades of the desert can be in Summer. Learned how to ride a motorbike. How to fall off."

"I thought you were meant to stay on it?" She looked up at me. "I mean, if you're, like, good at it or something."

"Cheeky," I reprimanded her to the sweet chorus of her giggle. "Knowing how to fall off is important. If you do it wrong, you might not have the chance to get back on and ride again."

She chewed that slowly over for another minute. "You are the philosopher," she murmured as we turned into the park.

"I did three courses at college," I admitted, "if only to annoy my old man who wanted me to become an accountant."

"I take it that didn't happen." She grinned, kicking at a small snowdrift and nearly fell over herself.

"Whoa, girl." I held on tighter and set her back on her feet. "Don't attack snow that hasn't done anything to you." The snow had stopped for the moment, but the clouds overhead felt heavy and pregnant, rather than little fluffy bunnies. Mind, there was plenty of the stuff on the ground to cater for my needs. "No, I didn't do accounting. I studied economics, and people. Critical thinking, again to annoy my father."

"What does he think of you now?" She rose on her toes to kiss me and missed by most of a mile.

"Jesus." I shook my head, snorted and planted my mouth over hers. What started as a smooch devolved into something pornographic in moments. "I swear I'll never get used to the taste of you."

Her eyes were sad when I drew back, and I cursed myself from bringing up our shortened time again.

"My father passed away a few years ago. Mom's in a home in Sydney. Dementia." I shot her a look when her eyes filled with tears. "Don't," I said gently. "Right now she thinks she's a teen most days, dating my father. They had that sort of relationship that started in high school and lasted forever," I said wistfully. "As far as I can tell, they're dating right now, in her mind. She rarely drifts back any more and talks about him incessantly. I know more about that first date than I need," I said wryly.

"X rated?" Nisha affected a look of horror.

"He was the cheesiest," I admitted.

"Gee, something you have in common," she grinned playfully.

"Thanks. I aim to please," I said with a straight face. Just.

Noisha giggled, then sighed. "You're lucky to have a family."

"You don't?" I clung to each word, eager to know more about the girl than the facade she showed the world.

"They got divorced when I was sixteen. Mom went to DC as a partner in a law firm Dad disappeared into Canada as a travelling musician. I didn't want to leave here. It's the only place I've ever lived and something about the city is the best thing in my life...you know," she mumbled, biting her lip and studying her snow covered boots. "I studied art at NYU after, and my best friend's mother took me in for my final years at high school. So I studied, I fell apart, reinvented myself, got crappy jobs and decided I'd do my own thing after something I love. So my form of art is showing the city to those who see it through a screen or in a magazine and making it that much more real. Which usually leaves me a few bucks short of broke. Stupid, huh? I should be displaying oils in a gallery but…then I'd miss this." She waved her gloved hands around her at the snow covered vista the park presented.

People milled about everywhere, and we followed different sets of footsteps that veered off the path, winding our own way into fresh snow beneath a copse of trees laden with tiny icicles that reflected an inverted city view.

"It's not silly. You love the people and the city…I'd say you're doing what you were always meant to do," I murmured, a mad, Millham-level crazy idea forming inside my head.

"My bank account says otherwise," Nisha muttered. "But hey, I have a ham and I'm baking it for breakfast tomorrow."

"You're baking a ham for breakfast?" I repeated. "Is that a NYC thing?"

"It's a Nisha thing." She shrugged. "I cook for the super of my building and a few others who are city orphans like me. We make an odd little family, drink, talk, eat too much and wander off sometime in the afternoon to nap. It's kinda perfect," she admitted, sliding her gaze up to me. "You wanna come hang out in my dingy apartment for Christmas?"

"Nothing I'd like better," I said honestly when her mouth fell open. I kissed her again, addicted to the feel of her mouth beneath mine.

"Okay." Her whisper filled with a sense of awe. "You weren't part of my Christmas plan, you know."

"You had one of those?" I grinned when she slapped my coat. "Not even gonna pretend to say ow."

"I plan. Stuff just doesn't always stick to you, you know." She frowned. "Why are you laughing at me?"

"Because you're so damn cute it hurts." I wrapped an arm around her waist, and pulled her into the snow.

Nisha shrieked, but we were far enough off the path that

the only few passerbys laughed as I rolled us on our backs and patted the snow from her face. "Oops. Didn't mean to make you a snow man."

"Uh uh," she muttered. "Hope you like it cold, Aussie." She stuffed a handful of fresh snow down the front of my jacket.

I howled for her amusement, though the cold felt good against the faded sting of the tattoo.

The things that have happened this Christmas.

I turned off my phone most of the time, taking the ridiculously overdue break from my business. And Nisha was the perfect foil. "Don't fight with a man who has larger hands than you do," I warned, scooping snow between my fingers. I ducked the snowball she aimed at me that shattered on a branch overhead. "Missed."

"No, I didn't." She giggled as everything on the branch and the one above that deluged right on my head. "Cute, huh?"

I formed the fastest, largest snowball I could and tossed it straight at her head.

She didn't duck in time.

I laughed, shocking the snow off me as a tiny tile of snow dusted her nose. "Damn right you're cute. Come here."

"No way." She darted off as I rolled to one side, grabbing her waist as she shot by much slower than I suspected she intended.

Nisha fell against me, our clothes starting to soak through but I didn't care. The bath in the suite was big enough for both of us to eke the cold out later.

"You're so not getting away." I formed a scoop with my fingers, letting the crystals trickle into the front of her jacket.

"Oh, fuck!" she cussed, her eyes open wide.

I laughed until my stomach ached with it, intent on covering her with snow—which I succeeded in a few times—though I ended up wearing my fair share. Nisha had good aim when there wasn't a snowball coming her away.

"Sure you didn't grow up playing little league," I gasped, tugging her to my chest and falling on my back in the disturbed now. "Perfect."

I rolled her off me and waved my arms and legs around.

"What are you doing, you crazy man?" She laughed at me, half sitting up.

"It's obvious." I pretend her comment hurts, wrinkling my nose.

She matched me, squinted eyes and all, until she earned another laugh out of me. "No, it's not."

"Snow elves." I sighed. "What am I going to do with you, Nisha?"

She giggled, lying down and copying me, both of us waving our limbs about in the snow like six year olds on a snow day.

Except I knew the answer to my own question.

I wanted to keep her.

Forever.

"OH GOD, THAT FEELS GOOD."

She sank so deep into the water so the only thing I could see were her eyes peering at me through thick lashes. Her halo of raven black hair floated around her. I pushed my thighs to the sides of the bath, reaching out to catch one of the blue black locks and tugged her towards me until she kneeled close enough to touch.

"Feel better?"

"Much." She swatted in the steaming water just out of my reach, the water lapping her skin provocatively.

Three minutes into the bubble bath I couldn't keep my hands off her, gripping her hips and pulling her onto my, syncing the natural sway of her body against mine. The additional contact and heat left me breathless.

"Yeah," I managed in a strangled voice. "What were we talking about?"

Nisha wiggles hips thoughtfully. Her breasts rose out of the water with each inhale, then disappearing into the bubbles, the dusky skin of her nipples visible.

I thanked the hot water for her extra sensitivity, tracing gently over her reddened skin, skating my fingers a little closer to where her thighs spread over me, drawing her closer, because her flesh wasn't the only one responding to the proximity. The pins and needles tingle in my fingers evaporate at the moment she touched me, sliding her hands around my shoulders and massaging muscles there.

"Jesus. I am keeping you forever." I tipped my head backwards, my eyes closed, so I didn't have to see her reaction to my words.

Because all of me, not even a little bit in the negative, wanted that statement to be true.

I choose my own fate.

I always had, since college. Rooming with Rex, a full day's flight away from home and the natural apron strings set something alight in my bloodstream. Something addictive.

Closing my hands around her ribs, I grazed my palms upward until her heavy breasts filled my palms.

"Tell me you're okay?" I asked when she whimpered something. Her mouth brushed mine in a feather-like kiss, while all my remaining blood hurtled south.

"Yeah," she whispered. "I've barely touched you. Did you know that?"

Her gaze flitted down, following the trajectory of her hand as she reached between my legs, finding my erect cock, and squeezed.

A groan ripped from my mouth. "I don't think I had." A great oversight I have to fix next time.

Will there be a next time?

"I've had the shot," she said, hopefully.

I was content to blame my cock cock for stealing rational thoughts from my brain. "Good enough for me." I cupped my hands around her hips, lowering her slowly, and slid inside her.

Nisha hung there, suspended in the hot, foaming water, all splayed wide and tender for me. Her soft breaths were my heart song as she closed around me, and I pushed up, stealing her cries to savor once more. Closing my mouth over hers, I thrust my tongue inside her to taste.

Berries, fresh snow flakes, and fairy lights on Christmas trees.

Everything about Christmas I never understood as a kid, the magic washed away by an all too early adulthood that had nothing to do with who I was.

Nisha held all the things missing in my own life.

Her soft cries filled my head with dreamsI couldn't have. Pushing down hard, I thrust recklessly inside her. Her moans mixed with slushy water, bubbles creeping up over the edges of her breasts to drop into the valley between. I leaned my head back and pulsed my hips inside her.

My girl gave as good as she got, rolling her hips back into me, her nails digging into my shoulders as her pussy tightened around me.

"That's it, princess," I purred, remembering how much she liked my dirty talk before. Two days to get to this. Hell, it can't have only been two days. Three days. Fuck it, who cares."

Her musical cries edged us both as I worked my hips harder while my Chrtostmas present this year was Nisha unravelling around me. Her sounds perfect and her hot little pussy clenching around my cock, I groaned as she milked me and we came together in seconds. All the teasing, feeling all loved up, the last hours were everything that washed over us in a tsunami of Christmas morning desires. I stared down at the mess we made of the bathroom and didn't care. Not because someone had to clean it up, but because Nisha responded to me the same way I felt about her.

My dozy girl rested her head against my shoulder. The toxic doubt that worried me dissipated with nowhere to go as she licked sweat from my skin, humming and snoozing deeper with every touch and kiss. As I held her to me. No condom this time, something I'd never done before, though I loved the fact that I could feel everything. The way she fluttered around me, the tiny after-shocks, her writhing in pleasure we found new ways to torture each other.

Sweeping the bubbles around her body like a light blanket, I tugged her against my body, my limbs languid for the next hours when we didn't need to move. Nisha curled in my arms, her breaths puffing gently on my shoulder until the water cooled. Then I drew us both from the water, doing my best not to disturb her, towelling us off without parting from her body.

I laid her on the bed, kissing her swollen lips and woke her with gentle thrusts, my cock still hard inside her, needing to eke out every cry, commiting each into my memory, the taste of her, \as she came for me again and again.

Because like Cinderella at midnight, though I didn't know it yet, she was gone.

CHAPTER 11

NISHA

I STARTED COOKING my Christmas ham at 3 am.

It took me long enough to extract myself from beneath Ford, this time sliding on my elf tights and back into my familiar jacket. The scent of him seemed imprinted on me after we made love again, like darkened mornings replaced with a glittering darkness of Christmas promises.

A promise I broke when I stepped outside his door at the Plaza and let it close behind me, leaving my key in the things he bought me on the bedside table.

Doubling down on my dose of guilt, I stepped out of the Plaza to hail a cab in the longest, heaviest walk I had ever taken. My legs trembled as I curled on the stained back seat of the yellow taxi, staring through slightly smoky tinted windows as the city lights merged to a stream of Christmas colours and glitter.

My apartment building was quiet when I got home, and, after sitting on the edge of my bed, staring at my hands for more than an hour, I got up and started to prepare everything for breakfast the next morning.

Thankfully, for me, preparing for Christmas usually took me the night before to prep, and I had sleepless hours to fill. Usually I lost myself in mixing the sauces, prepping the ham and slicing it into neat diamonds and matching the cherries to each space. But this time, every movement was robotic.

Ford promised things all too easy that couldn't possibly come true and I couldn't bear that. Actually, my heart couldn't bear any of it. Because in two or three days time he would leave, and I would never see him again.

For my heart's sake I couldn't have that door left open every time I thought of his stupid, muscular pecs with his alpaca's face tattooed there. And the only way to avoid feeling was to end it on my own terms. No surprises for me. And so I wound my arms around myself and sipped the red wine that sat on my counter, for how long. I hadn't been saving it, I just never had the time or the energy to drink water.

Now, exhaustion no longer slammed into me the way it did on a daily basis last year, as a Band-Aid fix for the hollow spaces etched inside me.

And every single one of those hollow spaces was filled with the same thing:.

A void of Ford Millham scented nothingness.

I didn't know if the wind helped or not, but I continued cooking until my apartment smelled like Christmas. By the time that first neighbors arrived at seven am, my small table and counters were full of heaped platters. The ham was decorated with perfect diamonds and glace cherries. Mountains of candied oranges and steamed vegetables, honey baby carrots, and green filled the others to create a feast, worthy of the king of our building.

"You've done me proud, Nisha." Jeremiah sniffed

appreciatively at the collection of plates displayed as he waddled with in a slightly limp his right side.

"Did you fall? Did you get up another ladder, Jeremih?" I threw a hand on my hip and popped it out.

"Don't give me sass, girl. It's Christmas."

"All the more reason for it." I gave him a giant hug until he wheezed faintly. "Merry Christmas Jeremiah." I reached around my fridge for the small collection of presents there and collected a smallbox.

"I knew she was going to pop the question," he joked to the small collection of neighbours filing in behind him.

"You still haven't told me how you fell off that ladder," I called,l heading back to the kitchen for the giant ham and the knife I sharpened earlier.

"It was only the second rum, and the other window needed fixing." Jeremih glared at me. "You tricked me." He unwrapped his present. "Which is a…" He turned the black silicon rectangle around and looked up at me in desperation.

I grinned. "It's a reading light. See?" I showed him how to work the flexible silicon and touched the back of the light, where a small bulb glowed. "It's not too heavy, which means you can use it with your paper. No more ladders for a while though."

Jeremiah was still for a moment.

"If it's not right, I'll swap for something else," I worried.

Jeremian wrapped his arms around me, and I was engulfed in cinnamon and cigar.

"Thank you," Jeremiah said meekly.

At the other end of the table, someone started humming 'Jeremiah was a bullfrog'.

Unable to take any additional doses of emotion, I counted my stack of plates, and grabbed two, handing them out. Denise took one with a grin and a quick *merry Christmas, bitch.*

"Help yourself. I made enough for the army, and I don't expect anyone to fall asleep until midday."

A hard rap on the door roused me out of my ham-induced haze. I popped a glace cherry into my mouth as my door cracked on its hinges.

"Jeremiah, could you help whoever that was? Sally's missing. And Mr Andrews from the top floor. I'll go check on him in a minute if he doesn't come down."

Jonathan Andrews wasn't so sprightly at a solid one hundred and two years old, though the grumpy old man seemed intent on staying on the top floor until the last day of his life.

"Long as he's not stuck again," Jeremiah said, heading for my small entryway blocked from the kitchen and combined living area. "Ah."

"It sticks," I yelled over my shoulder, placing overloaded plates in front of Denise and her nearest neighbour Gerard.

"Looks amazing, Nisha," Denise wiggled in her seat. "You've gotta tell me where you've been the last few days."

"It's a tale," I answered softly, avoiding details as my heart clenched and I closed my mouth.

Denise eyed me speculatively, and started with a chunk of Christmas cake I placed in front of her without a word.

Another knock from the region of my door.

"Give it a kick at the bottom right," I yelled, hopefully. "A really hard one. It's stubborn."

"No kidding." A deep voice I'd recognise anywhere filled my small apartment, the same way as it had to the bottom floor of the Plaza Hotel the day he decided to spout off about appendages and ugly sweater socks.

I closed my eyes, pushing the tears backwards, and managed to not fall off the floor as I thought I might.

"You know, I can help you with that," Ford's voice reached me from far away.

"Appreciate it. Might need a replacement."

They're talking about the door. I picked out Jeremiah's voice mixed with my lover of the moment.

Oh hell, that's weird.

The admission *did* feel weird. I hadn't had a date for years, just as I told Ford.

"I'll get you something tomorrow."

Jeremiah muttered something back and Ford seemed to disappear for a minute.

Gerard pushed back from his seat, chair, scraping horribly on linoleum. "Is there someone I need to kick out?" He asked softly, on my side, carrying a plate of candied oranges. "I've still got the goods."

I smiled weakly. "You might have been a cop once upon a time, but I'm not sure you can take that man."

"Man?" Gerard looked at me sideways. "I meant the fuzzy-looking beast."

Pickles stood in the middle of my living area, his back hooves on his very own piece of newspaper.

"Nobody brings an alpaca to Christmas," I whispered.

A Santa hat slanted rakishly across the stud alpaca's head, and candy cane dangled from his halter.

"Who doesn't?" Ford appeared in the doorway, holding a spare Santa hat, leaning back against the doorframe, the picture of relaxation. "Hi, Nisha."

Butterflies wound through my stomach, the reindeers giving it a break for the day. Every set of eyes around my table made their way to me, waiting.

I had absolutely nothing.

"Who's this–?" Denise reached back to ruffle Pickles' fuzz.

"This is Pickles. The alpaca." *Thank you, Captain Obvious.* "And Ford. He's…" I shook my head. Did I want him to be here? I gazed at Pickles and then closed my eyes, then found Ford smiling at me like a loon.

Do you want me to go? he mouthed.

I shook my head, gripping the counter tight. *No.* It was all I had, nothing else.

That red wine is really taking effect right now. I halted that path of thought, only realising I'd spoken out loud when the entire kitchen burst into laughter.

Denise got up, snuggling Pickles, while Jeremiah took a discreet step back in the wrong direction. Pickles' throat worked the wrong way.

"Yeah, watch out for that." I left the super to deal with Pickles on his own and faced Ford.

There was a joke there, but my idle brain couldn't pick it out.

Ford crossed my living space and kitchen into long strides, leaning down to brush his lips over mine. "Merry Christmas," he murmured.

I swooned, and straightened and slapped him and regretted it, anger busting out of me in the climax of the grieving circle in a matter of seconds.

Ford didn't move an inch, giving me a hard look I knew I'd never forget. "You left. You know that puts you on the naughty list?"

"Does it?" I said faintly, wondering what the punishment was for earning myself a spot on that side of the list. A spanking? Or a lifetime of abandonment?

My heart tumbled a little inside my chest. "What are you doing here?"

"I was promised ham for breakfast." Ford smiled. "And I didn't have anything else to bring, except for...." A small, rectangular package wrapped in plain brown paper.

I shook my head. Ford gave me enough already, though I managed to return the goods. I didn't expect to do gifts with him, or anyone else.

My mind picked on the weirdest facts, clinging to some

semblance of reality I understood. "When did you fly to California and collect Pickles?"

He shook his head, still smiling. "He wasn't in Cali. He was getting his sperm frozen at an institution for a rainy day event. Also, I didn't intend to come back when I planned all this. That was before I had a reason to."

"Oh." *Eloquent, Nisha.*

"Something like that. Are you going to introduce me?"

Jerking a little, I did the rounds, staring at the package in my hands and back at Ford.

"Open it." Ford's lips brushed my ear, his soft whisper edging its way down my spine.

Turning the package over, I slipped open the neat sticky tape at the bottom of the pack working around its clean edges and straight lines, so very much Ford.

I held back a laugh as I tore the package open, staring at the long, brown cylinders with their pretty ribbon tie downs. "Are these – what are they?" I asked Ford, confused. "An Aussie Christmas thing?"

He snorted. "Kind of like you're ugly sweater thing. Trust me, we don't get it." He took one of the brown paper cylinders free and held it out. "It's a Christmas cracker."

"Oh, crackers." Gerard rubbed his hands together, reminiscently. "I haven't seen one of those since Glasgow."

"You know, Glasgow is full of psychopaths." Denise waggled a finger in his face.

"Only if you believe the results of those tests. The silly ones online." He paused for a moment. "And we're only a few percent higher than the rest of the population anyway."

"Whatever you say." Denise said, her hand wrapped around one of the crackers at the end like a telescope. "How does it work?"

Ford demonstrated, gripping one end and offering me the

other. He held up a finger. "On three, we pull. Anyone PTSD with gunfire?"

I stared at him. "Are you going to shoot me?"

"Not quite."

Negative chorus rumbled around the world room. Every eye is fixed on Ford and his magical Christmas device.

"Three, two, one –"

The Christmas cracker, living up to its name, exploded in a shower of soft confetti and glitter. Something plastic hit me in the nose.

"Ow." I rubbed the tip of my nose. "You shot me."

"Never said I wouldn't."

Pickles honked his disapproval and whuffled at a piece of yellow and pink crumpled paper that folded out to become a paper crown.

"Does he do this to you too? Did you spit at him?" I leaned closer to the alpaca. "Should I spit at him?"

"Well, that'll be a different sort of entertainment." Gerard winked at Ford, who watched me, his mouth curving upward with amusement.

The yellow crinkle paper crunched in my hands as I placed it on my head. I reached up to touch the fine headdress, and passed Ford a blue one he placed on his own head. "Your traditions are weird."

"Ugly sweaters," he reminded me.

"Cool," Denise, and I chorused, devolving into giggles.

"Jesus. When did you start drinking?" Ford asked.

I still went. "About an hour after I left last night?"

The room fell silent.

Ford rubbed, back of his neck. "About that."

Gerard and Denise burst into laughter. Jeremiah crossed his arms over his bulbous chest.

"You'll be looking after a girl," he rumbled.

"Promise," Ford said softly, sending another ripple straight down to my toes this time.

I bent down and picked up the little plastic thing that hit me in the nose. A small plastic green frog sat in my hand, and a little hard tab appeared where its tail should be. I placed it on the table, studying the hollow quarter worth of plastic frog. Ford leaned over and pushed the back of it helpfully. The frog launched across the table. Denise, who hadn't been watching, screeched and scattered.

Jeremih nearly fell off his chair laughing.

"Is there one of these in each of them?" Gerard asked eagerly, holding his hand out. For the next hour or more the Christmas crackers filled the room with popping pops and cracks, glitter, and flying plastic frogs. And everyone wore their Christmas crown while we demolished the ham until we were stuffed.

Finally, around lunchtime, Gerard stood, still sucking on a candied orange slice, his knees cracking audibly. "Son, I haven't had a laugh that good in decades. You really brought Christmas back for me. The only thing missing were the jokes."

"Never was any good at those," Ford apologized.

Denise shuffled over. "Merry Christmas, Nisha. It's your best one yet."

Gerard looked up at Ford and held out a handshake. "I sure hope you're here next year. Bring some culture back."

Ford sketched a salute. "Yes, sir."

Chairs scrapped my flooring as I picked up plates from the table, consolidating some of the leftovers and stuffing from the rolled turkey Denise brought down.

"And that's Christmas here." I smiled at Ford, the smile that slipped as he regarded me intensely. "What? Do I have a plastic frog on my face?"

"You're missing some of that reindeer face paint."

Denise and Gerard and Jeremih came in for a quiet round of hugs, each wishing a merry Christmas and thanking me for food. As I wrapped up leftovers Denise promised to take up to Sally and check on her, I placed one of the tiny gets on top.

"Please make sure she's okay, and if you need help come in for me."

Denise gave Pickles a friendly cuddle, dropping some carrots into his bucket.

"I'm not really sure he eats those."

Denise shrugged. "We'll find out."

"Merry Christmas."

"Are you going to be back on board after Christmas, or do you want me to keep up with your bookings?"

I closed my eyes and the words lodged in my throat. "I'll be back on board the twenty-seventh," I managed, even dropping a cheery note in there.

Denise's eyes narrowed, darting between the man on my back and my face. "Do you want to talk later?"

"See you on the twenty-seventh." My smile started to fall apart, the words burning the back of my tongue with bitter seeds.

"Yes, ma'am." Denise hugged me fiercely and nodded to Ford. "Merry Christmas," she said, with all the levity of a mafia Don proclaiming a family death.

"Merry Christmas," Ford echoed, as I closed the door behind Denise,

Suddenly, though I still had two guests, my small apartment was bereft of the noisy souls of the moment, before leaving me with an alpaca and his master.

I leaned my back to the door and closed my eyes. "I'm exhausted."

"You never got much sleep last night." Ford's fingers brushed across my waist. My breath hitched at his proximity. "From what it sounds like."

"Not much. Christmas probably goes a lot longer where you're from," I managed a grin. "But we're early risers, and now we kinda crash for the rest of the afternoon. Our own weird little Christmas Siesta."

I shut my mouth after that. All of us had to get back to work tomorrow and Jeremiah never really stopped. No doubt somebody would break or another door or the heating would go out or something.

Not everybody got to do anything they wanted over Christmas.

"Good."

"Good?" I cracked an eye and stared through the slanted lens at Ford. "Why is that good?"

"Because I've been waiting for hours to do this."

Two large, rough hands cupped my cheeks as he leaned in and pressed his mouth tenderly to mine.

Ignoring my breaking heart, I wound my arms around the back of his neck and let him kiss me until I could barely stand on my own. Pickles whickered softly in approval in the background.

And when Ford lifted me and his arms and carried me into my bedroom, I let him.

I SNORT SOFTLY in time with the rumble inside for the chest, my new favourite way to fall asleep. Something about doing absolutely nothing in the middle of the day brought back memories of my childhood that I either tried to forget or remembered everything, knowing I could never go back.

For a few short hours, Ford gave me that ability to sink back from the stress and the business of it all.

Right until my brain started working, finally processing the last days.

"Something," I rubbed my eyes, yawning. "I feel like I need to go back."

"You're not going anywhere, princess. You're all mine right now."

I smiled and pressed a kiss to his chest where we were both covered in drying sweat. "You're like a hot water bottle. And I can't just stop, you know?"

"Seriously? Are you fighting me, Nisha?" I could hear the smile in his voice, even if I didn't see it.

"No, I'm not fighting. But...at the wedding. Someone mentioned that you had a bet. That's why you need to date for the wedding."

Not that I saw him much for the entire time.

For trailed his fingertips along my spine beneath the quilt and blankets heaped around us like a giant nest. My entire apartment still smells like Christmas.

"That goddamn bet." Ford groaned.

"Was it with the other boys?"

"No, against the bridesmaids." He paused for a moment. "Who mentioned it to you?" he asked cautiously.

I closed my eyes. "Your ex."

"Fucking Jess. Am I never gonna be free of her?"

"I mean, we can concoct a plan," I added hopefully.

Ford tapped my nose. "Sassy." He drew me up in front of him until we were looking straight down the bridges of our noses. "What do you need to know?"

It wasn't said with resignation, more a serious question, like he really did want to alleviate my fears.

What did I have the right to ask? This was the temporary fixture. He couldn't be here after tomorrow. The day after.

Still...

"I just wondered what the bet was."

"We had to have a date for the wedding. Originally we were going with the bridesmaids, but that turned out to be a bad idea, and then there was a bit of alcohol and a mother of the groom involved."

"So... You just made it out to be something painful right?" My voice rose a little at the end. I closed my mouth and stopped speaking.

Ford's hand clasped around the back of my head and he never lost his sombre expression. "I didn't ask you because I needed a date. I asked because I didn't want to spend time without you. We crashed into each other and I didn't want to lose the chaos that follows you around to stop. Nisha, I exist in a strictly organised world. I haven't had a break in over a decade and you're just," his eyes ran to my face, and he tugged me a little closer until his lips grazed mine when he spoke, "perfect."

"So are you," I said, without thinking, and closed my eyes. "I'm sorry. I shouldn't –"

"We both shouldn't, Nisha, but I think this is gonna happen." Ford gave me a goofy grin I was starting to warm to when I peeked at him. "Whether we want to or not. Though three days is a record for me."

"Two days." It was the point I couldn't get past. "If you come back to America more often, maybe we could…"

Outside my bedroom, Pickles honked.

"Privacy. Have a thought and go back to your newspaper," I called the alpaca.

Pickles waffled in the kitchen and I wondered how much of the leftovers remained.

Ford's fingers rub circles at the back of my head. "We can make it work," he insisted.

"Can we?" I offered a soft laugh that did not hold any humour. "I don't fit into your world, Ford. No matter how much I want to."

My door pounded, or someone on the other side of it did.

"Will this always happen, too?" he inquired softly.

I dropped my forehead to thump his chest. "Most likely."

"Nisha, Ford!" Denise shouted. "Get your butts out here."

I lifted my face from the warmth of his chest, reading the resignation there, but my brain wasn't in gear enough to process anything. I scrambled to my feet, grabbing my yoga pants and a sweatshirt and threw a hoodie over the lot. "Is it Sally?" I puffed, sliding into the kitchen. "Is she okay? Christ, did she die?"

It took me a hard kick and a few tugs with Denise pushing on the other side until she tumbled into me, breathless and red-faced, but eventually the door did open. When she looked up, her eyes were wide and excited. "No! It's the media. There's a camera crew camped out the front and more arriving."

"Really? Did we break a law or something?"

"You didn't do anything."

Ford stepped out of my bedroom, already in his jeans and boots, buttoning up the shirt.

Denise shot a triumphant look between myself and Ford. " I knew it!"

"Stop that," I shushed her.

"It's this." Ford held out his phone. I took it while he finished putting his shirt on and slid into his jacket. He wound hard arms around me and pressed a kiss to the top of my head. "I should go. They'll follow me, keep their eyes off you guys. Works most times."

I read the message on this phone, barely able to make sense of the words. "Why is your ex asking you to call Richard?"

"Richard Martin. The one who served Jess ages ago. I should've done that AVO." Ford kissed me, and I felt the possession with every indecent sweep of his tongue inside my mouth. "I didn't want to leave it this way."

"What's happening?"

Denise drew in a sharp breath. "Oh, my God."

I twisted between them. "What. Is. It? Before I castrate someone?"

Pickles edged away, the whites of his eyes showing.

Ford and Denise held a silent conversation over my head.

"I'll tell her," Denise finally promised.

"I'm sorry." Ford cupped my face and kissed me hard, leaving my head spinning with the scent of Christmas and him and heartbreak.

"Don't make this goodbye," I whispered, out of my realm, my depth, of everything.

"I – I don't know when I'll see you. But this has been incredible. It's not how I wanted to leave it." He stared at me hard for a long moment, and then pushed around Denise, grabbing Pickles by the halter and strode out the door, leaving me alone.

I didn't even have time to ask how they managed the stairs.

My apartment lost two more souls.

I blinked at the empty space, wrapping my arms around myself. "I'm lost."

Denise launched onto me in a huge hug. "We need to have a bird and the bees talk, babe. He's Ford Millham, isn't he?"

"Yes." I frowned. "How did you know?"

She sighed. "Because he owns FCMC." Her sigh hit double strength as she shook her head when I didn't even flinch. "Wake up, Nisha! The big green and yellow building we thought was getting sold, because of some personal thing. With the dust when it was getting built, the dust we bitched about for freaking months. And the gold gilt toilet rumours," she added when I watched her blankly.

"No freaking way. He's one of the wealthiest men in New York."

"Yes, he is, darling. And I think the media followed him here."

I shook my head. "His ex. She's been up his butt about their break up this time last year and claiming monies owed or something. Drama llamas." I swallowed. "He– we were talking about doing a long distance thing. I think. But that seemed, you know, final."

"It did." Denise nodded. "And you have his number, right?"

"Ah, no?" The first tears started to fall. "No, I don't."

The sympathetic look Denise gave me was too much. I marched into the kitchen, grabbed the nearest plate of leftovers, and a fork.

Not saying a word, Denise picked up the other plate and extracted a bottle of Beam from somewhere, twisting the cap off and holding it out the moment my butt hit the worn sofa.

My perfect Christmas devolved into yet another memory I knew I'd push aside every year right along with all the others I didn't want to remember.

CHAPTER 12

NISHA

I WORKED December twenty-sixth nursing a massive hangover and cursing into my mic as I wound my way between shop owners and workmen, taking down the slightly wilted plastic trees and decorations around the city, replacing them with the promise of glimmering, glitzy new things for the new year.

No phone calls or messages from different numbers, no sense of Ford anywhere. The FCMC building–Ford Colton–his deceased brother, I learned through an internet search–Millham and Co never went up for sale, its owner still as elusive as ever, having disappeared and taking his mini media storm with him. They never returned to my apartment block, thankfully, though Jeremiah kept a steady watch each morning.

Denise wanted to share my tour shifts in a bid to let me grieve for my heart, but I needed to keep busy. By the time I said farewell to my slightly dazed tour, collecting my tips and stuffing them in my pocket though Ford's payout made them obsolete for now, my feet ached, I limped a little as I pushed my weary limbs back to my apartment. I barely had the energy to say hello to Jeremiah, and Denise was still out when I collapsed on my bed without undressing and snoring my way through until dawn.

Rinse and repeat.

All the way right up until New Year's Eve.

Not that much changed as I collected my tips that afternoon, slightly numb and absently wishing everyone a Happy New Year, though I might have slipped a few 'merry Christmases' in there by accident from some of the odd looks I got.

Meh. Not that it mattered. I wasn't seeing any of these people again. The attitude I always hated in tour guides that came back to haunt me. But the same values I clung to no longer mattered as much. I did my tours with the bare minimum, all the same spiel, none of the same heart.

That went home on the back of an alpaca riding off into the sunset, or some such bullshit. My heart hurt too much to take on extra weight.

Cash was stuffed into my hand, a tiny lady poking me. "Next time, speak up!" she yelled in my face, pointing to her hearing aid.

I leaned around her, studying the tiny contraption and wiggled my fingers near her ear. She nodded and I squeezed the bottom of the device, the battery door clicking into place. "Better?"

She nodded, a wide grin on her face and patted me, pushing a few extra notes into my hand. "Thank you!" she yelled again, rubbing her ear.

"You're welcome," I said, bemused, the world suddenly less muted and more real, as though my own device had finally switched on, too.

"Good to know you're still helping out strays," a deep voice said behind me.

The world froze. A single snowflake drifted between us as I turned to face Ford, wearing the same shirt he had the day he left my apartment, standing there with his hands in his pockets and a cautious, albeit goofy grin spreading across his face as he looked at me like it was the most natural thing in all the world.

"I should slap you," I whispered.

Ford winced. "I deserve that. But let's do it in private, yeah? Dole out all the punishment you like, elf girl. But I can't deal with any more legal action right now."

I frowned. "What happened?"

"I settled with Jess."

My mind blanked, my bloodstream replaced by an influx of fast moving snowflakes. "You settled. So what are you doing here if you're with her?"

"Huh?" Ford started. "Jesus, princess. I settled. Out of court," he said slowly. "As in I paid her a ludicrous sum to fuck right off and never come back at me again."

"You. Bribed. Her." But he wasn't with her. I heard that right. But also, he left and I should have slapped him. Right? Or maybe kiss and slap? What was the standard here?

"She tried to blackmail me. It hurts less this way. But if I have to read another contract in the next forty-eight hours my head will actually explode." He tried for a grin again, the fine lines around his mouth straining its edges.

"At least implode. You'll make less mess that way," I promised him. "Gotta think of others. And I thought you went home on the twenty-seventh?"

"I never left, Neesh. I've been here fixing things the entire time. And I've stood there, across the road, watching you start and finish your tour every day like a good little stalker," he said seriously.

"You have?" I stared. If I did it any more my eyeballs would pop out on their stalks and wave hello to him in person.

"Sure have." He took a slow step forward. People milled around us, their heads down as the snow started up. "Left Pickles at home. Not that he's impressed. He looks good in sunglasses."

A snort escaped me. "So incognito."

"That's what he said." Ford paused, rubbing the back of his neck. "We didn't leave on good terms. Or any terms, really."

"You mean you didn't leave on any terms," I said tartly, stuffing my tips into my pouch. "That's what happened, Ford. You left me with no way to contact you, and you had my card. You could have messaged, or called, or *something*." I stamped a foot, sending up a flurry that turned to slush around my boot. "I'm tired, I'm hungry, and I want to go home."

I sounded like a petulant child who didn't know what she wanted but I didn't care. What I wanted was to forget I ever met Ford Millham.

Liar.

"Any chance I can help with that?" Ford pressed his lips into a hard line. "I want to make up for hurting you."

I spun around in a little circle, not really having any idea where I was headed. "Ford, I haven't gotten over the hurt of not being able to have you in my life. A few weird and wonderful and intense days...and nothing. My mind..." I made a puffing gestion, breaking my palms apart in a silent explosion. "And to go back through that and have you leave? I can't." My voice cracked as he stared at me, unmoving, unspeaking.

"About that. I'm uh, not going back. To Australia. Not for a while, anyway. And when I do it will be shorter trips. I'd like you to come with me."

"For your business trips? Are you mad?"

"Yes to the last, yes to the first but only as much as you'll stay with me the rest of the time while I'm in the States, Neesh. I don't want this to stop. And I know you love New York. I'd never willingly pull you out of it, except maybe for some short breaks. So, I figured if I wanted you, I had to move here. I got a five year visa. Kinda pushed it through."

"More bribes, huh?" I rolled my eyes.

Ford grimaced. "This one was a favour owed. But call it what you want. I'm here for a while, and if I can make it permanent, I'll do it."

"So you're staying." I nodded like it all made sense. Spoilers: inside my head, nothing at all was making sense.

"Yeah. I'm staying, princess. And I'd like to prove or disprove the theory of whether I shit in a golden toilet."

I narrowed my eyes. "So which one is it?"

He held out his hand. "You have to come with me to find out." His smile was lopsided as I studied his calluses that I secretly adored

"Mmm, okay. If only to find out about the toilet." I placed my hand in his.

"Is that the only reason, elf girl?" He pulled me straight into his chest, lowering his mouth and pausing just shy of making contact. "If I told you I loved you and got down on one knee, would you…"

"Slap you and call you a loon and make more legal problems for you?" I supplied. "Absofreakinlutely, Mister Millham."

"Good to know we're on the same page then." His arms wound around me tight, but it didn't feel like a cage, more of a safety net I desperately wanted to rely on. "Because I fell in love with you the moment you patted my alpaca, Nisha," he husked in his ear.

I giggled like a drunken elf who couldn't believe Christmas was actually over. "He was very cute," I said solemnly, managing to hold my face straight while my heart soared.

"Ford Millham loves me. That was what you just said, right?" I peered up at him. "Cute pets aside, you are telling me you love me and all the things?"

"All the things." He grazed his mouth across mine, lighting a string of fairy lights wrapped around my heart that wasn't going out when the clock hit midnight at new year.

"All the things."

"Except he's not a pet."

"If you say so. Let's go see these gold toilets."

"You're in for a dis–"

"Don't you dare spoil it," I warned him. "And you have a whole lot of making up to do. Just saying."

"Yes, ma'am."

And right there, with tourist cameras going off around us in a flurry of early fireworks, Ford kissed me soundly, and part of my heart glowed.

Okay, so the whole thing glowed. Because what he felt? I felt right back. Happy Chriastmas and Merry New Year to me.

Or something like that.

A NOTE ABOUT ALPACAS

Pickles came into the world because I have a female alpaca called Piccolo. The caramel, gorgeous girl is an Amazonian in her (smallish) herd and can't take a boy on board to actually bring out a baby. And because my then Mister 7 wanted to desperately call her baby Pickles, one that never seemed like it was ready to come out...you betcha. Alpacas in New York called Pickles. Complete with a Santa hat.

Honestly, that's how these things happen. A few extra alpaca facts:

Their necks can indeed be three feet long.

They have four stomachs.

That little bead when they are ready to spit is visible in a freshly shorn alpaca. Also watch the face.

Underbites are common. Don't let anyone tell you otherwise. The shearer will trim teeth and hooves before summer hits.

They can eat carrots and a few other veggies, though mine seem to love dried corn. Cut everything into small pieces to avoid the guzzle guts from choking.

They are super cuddly and also very skittish. When one freaks out, the entire herd goes along with it. They're also fiercely protective of their herd.

I am yet to get a Santa hat on my alpacas, but will try again this year at Lorendel Alpaca Park.

Want more of your favorite characters from the Betting on Christmas Collection?
Your authors all have created Bonus Scenes and Epilogues for you to revisit your characters and see how their stories continue.

A big city billionaire with a bride from a small twn. A high society New York City wedding with a momzilla being bossy boots. And a bridal party with one crazy bet. Will the bridesmaids and groomsmen find their own dates to the wedding of the century this Christmas, or will they all fall victim to Mozilla's decree?

Click here to find out in these **steamy holiday romances** from the **Betting On Christmas Collection.**

Prequel: **Betting on Christmas - The Bet**

BETTING ON CHRISTMAS

The Bride and Groom
It Happened One Christmas - Zee Irwin
The Bridesmaids
Who Needs A Boyfriend at Christmas - Delancey Stewart
Christmas & Other Inconveniences - Tracy Broemmer
Merry & Bright Christmas - Megan Ryder
Christmas with Her Fake Boyfriend - Kim Law
The Groomsmen
Mr. Grumpy's Christmas Date - Cat Johnson
He's Looking Like a Christmas Miracle - Amy Stephens
The Christmas Bargain - Peggy McKenzie
She's a Hot Christmas Mess - Sofia Aves
All I Want for Christmas is Her - Harper Cross

READ KING, Z BOYS

CHAPTER 1

KING

MY MARK WORE a pink and black chequered tie that clashed horribly with his date's dress. She, at least, exuded a dash of class. Even from my perch at the top of the residential block opposite the high end restaurant, I could see that.

My hands gripped at air, missing the familiar shape of my rifle, but I was under strict orders to leave it at home.

I could have as easily parted with my legs.

"Nothing." Scotty 'Joker' Evans rocked back onto his heels, jiggling about. Ever struggling with the serious side of our work, we could always rely on a smart ass comment from him in the midst of gunfire. Hence, his callsign.

We had all earned them, in one form or another.

"Sit still, you old bastard," I groused. "Don't they teach you anything useful in the RAF?"

"Piss off, King. You might actually learn something if you shut up once in a while." His British accent thickening, Joker gave me his trademark grin, one that many a lady—both young and not so young—dropped their knickers for.

I snorted softly, turning my attention back to the politician and his date. After his pedicure, he met her at his regular restaurant, not far from the expensive suite someone else rented for him.

The man wasn't influential yet, but he had the potential, which put him squarely on our radar.

Find out everything you can about him and file it for that rainy day when you'll need to use it.

Anything to protect the nation, even if it was several oceans away and twenty years in advance.

Joker continued to grumble beside me.

The politician—I winced again at his horrendous taste in ties—rose, tossing his napkin to the floor with disdain.

I zoomed in on my helmet display, studying her face, and then his. Had he hit her up for the night and she said no? He definitely misread that one.

His date folded her arms, looking away from him as a herd of waiters congregated about them. Even from the top of the next building, their fussing was overly pronounced.

I wondered if they were as keen to get Ugly Tie out of the restaurant as his date clearly intended.

A woman at the table behind turned to study the commotion, and I nearly dropped my kit.

Stunner.

Heavy lashes and dark, wavy chestnut hair were distinctly out of place in an exclusive restaurant in Cambodia. I shook my head, mentally tracing over her toned figure tucked into something red and sparkly.

Not the time or place, King.

My mark moved the fastest he had in weeks, and naturally I wasn't even watching him. He stormed through the restaurant's doors that were held open for him, the doormen bowing low. He sank into a car waiting at the curb, despite the fact his rented residence was only a three-block walk.

I tapped the radio at my side.

"Ugly Tie incoming. Same as usual." I smirked. It wasn't the first time my mark had left a date, though it *was* the first time she had kicked *him* out. I suspected his not-so-sweet talking skills had something to do with it. Or maybe he had terrible bedroom eyes.

"...the fuck? Reception's shit. Bald Eagle? ...moving?"

I snuffled a laugh. "Yeah. That one. See you back at the block."

***

"DON'T GO CHANGING designators over the radio, man." Lincon Kelly—*Ace*—berated me as soon as I stepped through the door of the holiday unit. The small section of Z-Unit cramped into a space that should have held four teenagers on schoolies at the absolute most.

Instead, three highly-trained military operatives hand-picked from their careers were stuffed into it, though technically, none of us existed on paper any more.

Wires and parts of computers lay in a haphazard mess strewn across the entire combined lounge and living area, surrounding the oversized mass of muscle planted in the centre.

"Fuck, it's like walking into Beruit." I stepped gingerly over some cords I thought weren't as critical and trod on some that were. Hearts moved and I flinched. "Seriously. Can't we look at these people before we name them? Ugly Tie is so much better than Bald fucking Eagle."

"We're naming *us* or anything that matters." Joker laid our surveillance kit on the table in a clatter of tech that hadn't been packed up properly.

"Damn, man." My flinch became a wince. "Will Mr Politician be replaced by the next gung-ho politician when he runs out of cash or sponsors? Yes. Will he run out of dates due to social ineptness? Also yes. Don't you ever feel sorry for these bastards?" I retraced my steps and claimed the bags of tech before Joker could damage anything further.

"You want me to feel sorry for a rich prick who bleeds poor people dry so he can live his rich prick lifestyle?" Hearts glared at me over his shoulder, pointing back the way I had come. "Plug that one back in. Talk about pricks," he muttered, tapping away frantically.

"How long do we keep tailing Ugly Tie?" Joker asked softly, running a hand through his hair.

I grinned. "I knew it would catch on."

"Seriously. The worst thing these local people do is poach from wildlife reserves because they're starving." Joker stuffed his hands into his pockets. "That's not a crime."

"Hell. You are in a mood."

"We've been here too long."

"You're a pair of whiny bitches. We're out in three days. Two more on recon, then we catch our flight home." Hearts shook his head, the behemoth of a man leaning forward, reading data from four screens at once.

"Home, man." Joker cheersed me with his water bottle.

I downed mine, and headed for the bedrooms.

"Where are you going?" Scotty called after me.

"I need to run."

Ignoring grumbles from the other two, I retreated into my spartan room and tugged off my protective vest, stripping back to bare skin. The kevlar didn't weigh much—and every one of us trained hundreds of hours wearing it—that it felt more naked without it than in it.

Every muscle had tightened with too many hours of surveillance. The inactivity killed me, in more ways than one, but at least I wasn't as fidgety as Joker. I trotted down the fire escape stairs, jumping the last few steps to hit the ground running.

Twenty blocks later, I turned around. Those same, tight muscles burning, I sprinted for as long as I could hold it before dropping back to a jog. The run wasn't just to keep my body going; the muscle that needed the most work was my brain.

Being cramped into a hotel room for nearly three months with only basic surveillance work came close to crippling me. My two hours out each night ate into my allocated sleep time, but my brain—and my body—were grateful for it.

Every inch of my body burned by the time I hit the fire escape for the return journey, my lungs sucking at air that wouldn't fill them as I sprinted the final flight.

The rest of my unit was already down by the time I crept back into the room.

———

TWO DAYS never seemed so long. Ugly Tie did his usual rounds both mornings, collecting his coffee and blow job from the delivery girl he under tipped for her tenacity and service under duress. Lunch was a simple affair involving lots of booze and too many associates who sat close together so there was no room for anyone to stab them in the back.

Dinner and another failed date.

On the second night, Ugly Tie stayed in.

"That's unusual." Hearts was still tapping at his keyboards in the apartment. "Stay with him, make sure nothing changes. Don't blow this on our last night. I'm keen to be on home soil." He punctuated his last words with a harsh tap.

Both Joker and I winced at the spliced static assailing our ears.

"He'd better do nothing." I adjusted the settings on my visor, but it didn't give me any greater insight on my mark.

"He's made two calls, hasn't eaten, and now..." Joker trailed off, squinting as he repeated my process, "he's going to bed? The hussies have worn him out."

"We're done, then." I stretched my calf slowly; the thing had gone to sleep beneath me.

We packed up in silence from then until we hit the street, the local night markets still active. Joker checked over his shoulder as he stepped out onto the street, jerking backward in a hurry as a tuk-tuk tore past him, a retro beatbox pounding in his wake.

"Hell, you do need to go home." I laughed as he cursed.

"Yeah, well. Home isn't home, is it?" he snapped cryptically, his cultured British accent thickening with his irritation. Finding a break in the traffic, he jogged across the road, leaving me on the other side.

The months we spent out of the country cost us plenty, but even so, none of us really had the lives others might expect. A regular special ops soldier might not be permitted to talk about his work, but to the rest of the world, Z Boys didn't exist.

Heading home did sound good, but Joker was right; we were headed for Australian soil. His home was halfway across the globe.

I inhaled my last few hours of Cambodia, relishing the lights and never-ceasing life of the place.

"ANY CHANCE you two can keep up?" Heart grunted as we headed for a small and inconsequential airfield.

Situated a few blocks from our hotel, it gave us a chance to hop onto a local charter and onto another, smaller plane to eventually land on military soil for our flight home.

Customs saw soldiers ready to head home, manifests provided from our cover unit dated months ago, and the pilots saw a pretty piece of paper with our false records, which they ignored.

"You make it sound like you're struggling, old man." I grinned at the big man's back, knowing he'd probably kick my ass the next time we trained together.

Which would probably be the day after we touched down on home ground.

Hearts had a good decade on me in skills and training, but my determination to push all his buttons equaled that.

"Just keep moving." Joker loped by me, his longer strides eating mine.

"Taking the order to *blend in* a little much, aren't you?"

The tall man's shoulders sloped, his back slightly bent, though his pack weighed little. Each of us had been in our civvies for so long, I knew it had begun to impact our mindset. Uniform was part of the training, part of the conditioning that kept us strong, focused.

I wondered if Joker remembered how to march. Ace would kick our backsides into gear in a few days.

We left the monotonous drone of the main streets behind, pushing through the outskirts of the town. Joker disappeared into foliage ahead, the track marked by a well-trodden patch of mud that disappeared between two trees.

A shadow passed across it, then another.

I frowned; neither were big enough to be one of my boys. Jogging the last few steps, I sloshed through the mud, a new drone filling my ears from the front. But the shadows disappeared across the foliage, not into the airfield beyond.

A handful of lean-to huts stood off to one side in a clearing, their occupants flitting about with menial, day-today tasks. A tiny figure darted into a hut, followed by a head of dark, chestnut waves.

My frown deepened. I glanced back to where Hearts and Joker had disappeared, but something drew me toward the lean-to.

Swearing softly, I slid the zip on my backpack, digging in to find my sidearm. I held it at my hip, fumbling with my other hand for the magazine.

The tiny hut was even tinier from the doorway. People scattered as I approached. Inside, a long-haired woman dressed in dark jeans and a rumpled tee huddled on the dirt floor in a hunched ball, talking quickly but soothingly to the shadow of a child I saw earlier. A satchel strung across her chest as she gestured to the child too fast for me to decipher their conversation.

A knot grew in my stomach as I realised they weren't alone. Money slipped from her hand to the child, who disappeared across the other side of the house and out through a window.

The woman turned to face the only other occupant, a man holding a matte black submachine gun aimed at her. He made a gesture with one hand, but she shook her head, clutching the strap of her laptop bag strung across her chest.

"At louy," she said in a clear voice.

No money.

I blinked. Reacting calmly in a shitty situation didn't come naturally to most people. It was something trained into your brain as you weighed the options in front of you with a clear assessment of what the outcome of each action would be.

Standing in the shadow outside the man's line of sight, I loaded my weapon and took another look at her.

I need to know who you are.

The ability to do that probably came down to how I dealt with the threat before me. In a darkened space on the outskirts of town, this was only going to end one way, and for the woman, it just came down to how messy the outcome was.

"She doesn't have any money." I held my arm just slightly behind me, as though reaching out to comfort her, edging into the hut. "You saw her give it away."

Large eyes swung my way, but I gave every inch of my attention to the man demanding it.

"I don't want her money." The man's English was better than I expected.

"Good. You hop out of here, honey," I said softly, flicking my finger behind my back.

Those eyes widened in my peripheral vision. The moment she began to move, I knew it was a shithouse idea to try to remove her from the situation she had gotten herself into without creating a greater threat than I could offer.

"Stay. Please." The man's cordial words were disputed by the jiggling of his weapon. A second armed man appeared from the other side of the hut—from a rear door, I assumed, since he didn't use the window the child had. Probably *why* the child had used the window as her exit strategy. This day was getting better and better.

I tried hard not to wince. "I need to take her home," I said firmly, sidestepping across the woman.

The tip of the gun followed my movement. Objective achieved.

More movement from the side of the hut I had entered from, but this time they were familiar shadows, which gave me additional options.

"She stays. Fun times." The man smiled.

I wished he hadn't. Several teeth were missing from it.

It was a moral choice on two fronts which may or may not have been altruistic. Save the girl, and fight the fight, because that was what we were trained for. And with his weapon aimed at me, I had a hall pass for what came next.

A simple aim and depression of the trigger.

And called that fateful word that would bring us all together.

I dropped to one knee.

"Contact."

Read King's story here

ABOUT THE AUTHOR

USA Today Bestselling author Sofia Aves writes fast-paced police romances, sizzling military units, steamy cowboys with a Montana backdrop and the occasional cheeky god. Married to a veteran, she often tackles topics of PTSD and reintegration and has a soft spot for all who work in uniform. Sofia writes kidlit for charity and has over one hundred and fifty publications across four not-so-super-secret pen names.

Sofia is a mum of three crazies in a returned veteran household and has an overly large fur baby who thinks she's a teacup puppy. After eighteen years of planning and dreaming, Sofia and her husband will put the finishing touches on their very own alpaca park this year. Sofia lives near Brisbane, Australia.

www.sofiaaves.com

Sign up to Sofia's newsletter and get a free Blue Blooded Brothers book.

Haven't read the Z Boy's prequel? Get it for free here:
A TABLE FOR TEN
www.sofiaves.com

Follow Sofia on
BookBub
Twitter
Instagram

Read Sofia's Series

Blue Blooded Brothers
Red Hart Ranch
Texan Devils
Z Boys
Sundae Dreaming
Australian Customs Security

Writing spicy paranormal romance as RAVEN HUSH
Club Fray
Monster Brides